PRISONER 1171

John Pascal

I the Lord have called you... to open eyes that are blind,
To free captives from prison, and to Release from the dungeon
Those who sit in darkness. Isa 42: 6-7

PRISONER 1171,

September 2014

ISBN: 13: 978-0692297735

10:0692297731

Third edition. Copyright pending

ACKNOWLEDGEMENTS

The author expresses his gratitude to his proof readers and to the San Diego Christian Writers Guild and its Temecula critique group hosted by Rebecca Farnbach. Also to the dedicated volunteers of Kairos Ministries for their advice and support.

All names and locations in this novel are fictitious and any resemblance to real persons and places is coincidental.

Our cover model is Rachel Leverenz, and her nasty bruise the work of Kayla Jones, a makeup artist on loan from the drama club of Fallbrook High School.

FORWARD

Prison--any prison--is a dark and dismal place, and, for many, a dead end. But it is never a place out of reach of the redeeming, life-giving love of God. Whether it is through staff members, outside volunteers, or another prisoner, the gift of hope and new life in Jesus Christ can be given, received, and nurtured, even there. As a longtime Kairos Prison Ministry volunteer and spiritual director, I've seen it happen. I've witnessed miracle after miracle in the lives of prisoners who were close to giving up. So, John Pascal's story of Esther Green Mason rings true. It's an engaging read and a powerful reminder of what can happen through the transforming love of God working in human lives.

While the novel itself is fiction, the mention of Kairos in the closing chapter is a reference to a very real ministry, dedicated to bringing light into the darkness of prison and generating the kind of life changes facilitated by Esther. Now active in over 400 prisons in 32 states and 9 countries outside the U.S., the stated mission of Kairos is "to bring Christ's love and forgiveness to all incarcerated individuals, the families, and those who work with them, and to assist in the transition to becoming productive citizens." Learn more at http://www.kairosprisonministry.org

Thomas Rothhaar, Spiritual Dir., Golden State Kairos, ret.

PART ONE

LAS VEGAS, NV

HOPELESS

"Este, they hurt you real bad if they catch you out there." Ginny searched Esther's gray-blue eyes trying to read her thoughts.

"Look, Honey, I gotta walk. I gotta think. I'm going crazy sitting in this trap of a mansion."

"But Jimmy, he real mad at you. I hear them talk."

"AArgh." Esther scratched her sandy-blonde hair with both hands and scowled. "Look, they killed my baby last month, Gin. Right now I don't care if they kill me next."

"B-but they might really, I think." Ginny grasped her shoulders. "I worry for you now."

"Ah, Gin, to Jimmy you're just his maid, but to me, you're my only friend."

Esther took hold of her hands and gently released her grasp. "Sorry, but I need some time away from here. I stole a key for the personnel gate. Just shut off the surveillance cameras. Remember, battery back up switch first, then pull the plug. Do some noisy cleanup near the kitchen to distract the cook."

"Okay, Este. I put red ribbon out your window if camera back on. 'Ten cuidado'."

Esther gave her a quick hug. "You're a sweetheart, Gin." She waited for Ginny to give her the thumbs up at the top of the stairs, and made for the sidewalk outside the gate.

The palms along the walk gave Esther some shade as she walked briskly along the suburban Las Vegas sidewalk. She took out a ball cap from her belt, gathered her short hair in it and pulled it on. *What I'd rather do is to just keep walking and never come back.*

She steadied her pace and began to breathe deeply but the sweet spring air did little to cheer her. *Seemed so good a few years back, didn't it? The end of foster homes: yea. I married a rich guy before I was twenty so I was supposed to start living the good life, right?*

After a few blocks she came to a corner bus stop with a covered bench and sat down. *Yeah, the good life, huh? Was I really so dumb not to realize this sweet talker was a mobster and I'd be a kept woman? Yeah, I was, but he didn't really lie, did he? I got a big house, fancy clothes, and two trips out to the mall every week. I can buy pretty much anything I want when I get there, but for what?*

Esther sat with her head drooped and watched a little speckled lizard skittering in the gutter. It came up and almost touched her pink jogging shoes before it ran off.

A bus pulled up and a Hispanic woman got off carrying a crocheted satchel. She smiled and nodded at her. Esther glanced up but didn't respond. *Sure, I can buy things and I get five hundred casino chips every week. Lots of fun at first, wasn't it? But now, I'd rather be back at my old foster home. At least I had some kind of family there.*

Her hands fell into her face and she began to sob. *Oh, my baby, my baby. What kind of a husband kills his child?*

A boy stopped his skateboard by the bench and flipped it upright with his foot. "You all right, lady?"

Esther sniffed hard and looked up. "Yeah, I'm fine. Thanks for asking." She wiped her tears off on her shirt sleeve and sniffed again. "I was just missing someone who died."

The skateboard came down with a bang. The boy shrugged and rolled off. "Bummer," he said.

Deep in thought, her gaze followed the tree-lined street and its wealthy homes. One house near the end of the next block stood out and caught her eye. It was a smallish wood frame house painted robin's egg blue with a white picket fence in front. She chuckled to herself. *That one looks like a TV set for a fifties sitcom and as out of place in this rich man's neighborhood as I am.*

Curious, Esther got up, crossed the street and walked down to get a closer look. A tabby cat sat just outside the fence, but he ran through the pickets when she came closer. She leaned against at the gate and admired the quaintness of the Victorianesque front porch. It lay partly hidden behind flowering bushes in front and wisteria vines dangling from the roof gutter.

"Oh, Hello, dear." Esther was startled by the voice. It came from the porch beyond the shrubbery.

She quickly pulled her hands off the gatepost. "Sorry, Ma'am, I didn't see you."

An elderly woman in a white dress limped to the top of the porch stairs to greet her. She was holding the tabby. "Dear, could you do a little favor for an old woman?"

"I, I guess so. What?"

"Some boys knocked this pot over, and it's too big for me to stand up."

Esther enjoyed the generous smile radiating from the top of the steps. It seemed to be part of the floral fragrance enveloping her yard. "Oh, sure, I guess."

Up on the porch she found a large square pot still holding a sideways date palm. She righted it with an "oomph," and swept up the spilled dirt with a nearby pan and broom.

"Thank you. That was sweet of you. I'm Lucia, by the way." That smile had to be returned.

Esther took her extended hand. "Esther, nice to meet'cha."

Lucia lowered her brows and peered into her eyes. "And you are a star indeed, just like your name, but I see you are deeply troubled, and I'll bet you are thirsty as well. The least I can do is offer you some lemonade and a little rest." She gestured to a porch table.

Esther turned to go. "No, that's okay but..." She paused. "I was gonna say I have to be going, but come to think of it, I've got nowhere to go."

Lucia laughed. "Then perhaps this is your destination."

Esther sat at the little table and poured lemonade into the two empty glasses next to the pitcher. Her expression became quizzical. "Your house looks different from everyone else around here."

"It was here long before the others. I wouldn't sell so the developers just built around it."

Esther's eyebrows went up. "Well, I think it's the cutest one around. Okay if I have one of those little cakes? I think I missed lunch today."

"Of course. They're for you." She pushed the plate toward her. "They're lemon crunch with chocolate bits. I made them this morning."

"Strange combo, Lucia, but darn good—creamy on the inside. Say, you know those brats who turned over your plant? How about I tell em what could happen to 'em next time?"

"That's very kind of you, but I let those boys play on my porch. Yesterday this place became a fort. You should have heard the gunfire," she chuckled.

"Yeah? But maybe they shouldn't have left you with a mess."

"I know, I know. They would have cleaned up but their stepdad across the street called them back with his police whistle. He's mean. Won't let them play in their own yard or even in the street."

Tabby cat had begun to rub against Esther's legs demanding attention. She stroked its back. "Lucia, you're a sweet lady, but tell me, how'd you get the idea I'm 'deeply troubled'?"

Lucia leaned sideways to check on her cat. "I see Miss Sassypants likes you. She has a sense about people too, but don't try and pick her up just yet."

Lucia quietly played with the edge of her ruffled sleeve for a moment, then leveled a look of concern. "It wasn't just your bloodshot eyes, Esther. God's given me a gift." She chuckled. "At least I *think* it's a gift. Sometimes I can discern unspoken things."

"So you're one of those who believe in God?"

"Believe? I prefer to call that a certain knowledge. God lives and loves. He listens and acts, and He loves you, my precious one, and hopes you receive Him in your heart."

Esther shifted around. *Uh oh, maybe I'm chatting with a crazy lady.* "Look, no one has *ever* loved me. I don't know much about God and I don't feel much like talking about it."

"Esther, dear, I understand. But will you indulge this old woman with a little bit of your time? No God talk, but you might feel better if you could talk about this thing that's making you so angry."

"Tell you—how'd you know that?"

"I sensed your anger when you put your hand on my gatepost, but I don't know what it's about. I also know you are a beautiful person, and I don't mean just on the outside. That's the obvious part. No, I mean on the *inside.* You might not guess it, but the Lord has a special plan for your life."

Esther gently nodded. "Okay, there's that God thing again. Look, I better get back before I'm missed." She stood up but became transfixed by Lucia's pleading expression.

Esther found herself saying, "But say, Lucia, maybe I *could* come back and talk more another time. You really wanna know why I'm pissed? No problem. I'll tell you."

"Yes, I really would love to hear why you're so angry. What time should I expect you?"

"Maybe seven tomorrow. Can't promise."

"That would be nice, dear. My schedule is, uh, flexible."

"Yeah, maybe I'll even let you tell me all about that plan God has for me. I just hope it's better than Jimmy's."

Lucia grinned. "Oh, it is, Esther. It is. I guarantee it."

CLOSE CALL

As Esther looked across the street from her house she saw the red ribbon being pulled in from her window. *Ginny must have seen me coming.*

She jogged over, opened the gate and hastened through the front door. "Ginny," she called out. "You up there?"

Ginny came thumping down the stairs, a scowl on her face. "You almost caught, Este. Cook just left. She might see you in street."

"Ahh, don't worry. I looked for the ribbon before I got close. Think she suspects anything?"

"You not come to dinner. She ask where you are."

Ester put her cap on a hook in the hall closet. "So, what did you tell her?"

"That you up in your room crying. Not to disturb."

"Good thinking, Honey. Not far from the truth these days. Cook serves dinner too early. I think she just wants to get home."

Ginny took off her work jacket and replaced it with a coat from the closet. "You know she report to Jimmy what you do. She left you dinner in fridge."

Esther gave her a quick hug. "Thanks for caring, Ginny. Sorry if I held you up too. I'll go back after supper tomorrow when I'm alone here."

Ginny's eyes widened. "Oh, no. You leave again? Jimmy has men that live near here. Now I worry more. Where you go?"

"I met the most interesting woman today, Gin. We just talked a little while, but I feel like we're old friends already." She pulled a booklet out of her jeans pocket and held it out. "Here, she gave me this to read."

Ginny took it and turned it over. "It the book of John."

"Yeah, she's all excited about God, like she knows he's real. You ever read any of this stuff?"

"Well—yes, but in our church we told the priest better tell us what it say."

Esther put a hand on her shoulder. "Hey, look, I'm keeping you from getting home. I'll study this John guy and maybe I'll be the one who tells you what he says."

INSPIRATION

The next day Lucia and Esther sat around a rusted, iron table that was sinking into the small lawn behind her house. Lucia had added puffy chair cushions for comfort and they sat under the shade of the neighbor's pepper tree. A chain link fence surrounded the yard, well covered with thick jasmine vines that afforded privacy and a pleasant aroma.

Esther patted her hand. "Lucia, you've put up with listening to my long song of woe, and I thank you for being patient. But what's *your* story?"

"Oh me? Not much to tell. I'm a widow. My husband was an investment banker and our only son died in Viet Nam. I had an unmarried sister who passed away a few years back, so all that's left is me, Sassy and the Lord."

"I can tell you're pretty relig…" Sassy bounded out of a hole under the fence and jumped up on Lucia's lap. "Whoa, talk about Sassy. She likes to visit your neighbor's yard, huh?"

"Oh yes. Cats don't follow people rules about their families. My little girl has two families. Sassy disappeared two years ago for a few days before I realized six-year-old Andy next door had adopted her too. Rather than plug up the hole, we agreed to share her."

Esther grinned. "Nice deal for kitty, but what if she just decided to stay on one side?"

Sassy found her shoulder blades being massaged and began to purr. "They feed her breakfast, and I give her dinner. I put in a pet door so she can come and go as she pleases."

"So she's got two families, huh. Nice life. I've never had one real family, Lucia. I don't count Jimmy's idea of one, and anyway he'll be either divorcing me or killing me soon. Right now I don't care which and, uh, I'm probably telling you more than I should."

Lucia nodded her head. "A pretty young girl like you? Don't speak nonsense. But if he's so foolish as to let you go, I'm sure you'll find the right man, hopefully one who wants children like you do."

"I doubt it. Men haven't exactly treated me well in the past, but you *had* a family and lost it. That's got to be worse."

Lucia dumped Sassy on the ground. "Can't spoil her too much. Well, you might not understand this right now, but I have a wonderful family in Christ. If you don't know the Lord it might seem crazy, but every day I have conversations with Jesus. He always listens, and sometimes he speaks to me as well. Also, my fellow Christians are like a family to me. One friend takes me to church and another one takes me shopping."

"Sorry but that sounds like dullsville."

"Nah, it's fun for an old cow like me. I take taxies all over the place too. That way I can be a reader to children in the library and visit people in the hospital. Stuff like that, and, of course, I do my share of telling others about Jesus. Did you read the booklet I gave you?"

"Yeah. I read it twice Seemed different the second time."

Lucia chuckled. "It was different?"

"Uh huh. On the second read I could feel the love coming out of it. But those guys didn't think Jesus was really God until the end, did they?"

"Yes, it's really hard for the natural mind, Esther. Believing this reality comes with something we call grace."

"Okay, it's interesting, I guess, but could we talk about it later?"

"Sure. I'd really love to welcome you into my family with Jesus, you know, save your soul as they say. But I won't scare you off. We'll wait until you're ready."

"Saved for what? A life with Jimmy?" She stared into Lucia's calm, resolute face. "Maybe some other time. Say, I noticed a violin hanging in your living room. You play that thing?"

"Not for years now, dear. With these arthritic hands I can't play very well but once a long time ago I was second violin in the Cleveland Symphony Orchestra."

"No kidding? That's so cool, Lucia. Are you in one of those old photos on your wall? I saw one with an orchestra."

"No, not me. They're even older than I am. I just love collecting historic photos. But say, let's do something fun. How about a game of scrabble?"

Esther shook her head. "I warn you, Lucia, I'm a writer and I know *lots* of words."

"Really? What do you write?"

"Children's stories."

"I think I'll beat the pants off you, little lady."

Esther laughed with a shriek. "Says *who?* Okay, you want to bet? If you lose you'll have to play me something on your old violin."

"I don't like betting, but say, if I *do* win, will you sincerely repeat a salvation prayer along with me?"

"You're on, grandma."

BABY STEPS

He will teach us his ways

So that we may walk in his paths. Isa 2: 3

After each visit, Esther looked forward even more to the next one. Today she walked down Lucia's street carrying a large plastic bag. As she got closer she could hear music, beautiful violin music.

She stood by the gate listening. A police whistle sounded from across the street and she heard a man shout: "Hey, lady, knock off the noise, will ya?" But the playing continued.

Lucia was sitting on her porch and she finished the last few notes with a fanfare. She looked up, saw Esther, and played the last few bars again. The man shouted at her again adding in profanity, but Lucia smiled and finished the piece. "There, did you like it?"

"Like it? That was crazy wonderful, Lucia. What's it called?"

"It's a little tune called 'Sicilienne,' but I have trouble playing the vibrato with my creaky joints. It sure isn't popular with him, is it?" She pointed her thumb across the street.

"Well, I love it, but why'd you decide to play?"

"Guilt."

"Really?"

"Yes. You should have challenged me on that triple word score a few weeks back."

Esther hopped up the stairs and gave her a hug. "So, it wasn't a real word?"

She chuckled. "*Always* challenge a strange, game-winning word. You've got nothing to lose."

Esther helped her get up and they went into the house. "The word sounded real."

"Ah, yes. And so do the words of a false prophet, only those words could kill you. What they say isn't in the Bible or from God, and my word isn't in the dictionary. You start reading the Bible I gave you?"

Esther took her package into the kitchen and turned to face her. "Uh huh. I've read Genesis, Isaiah and, of course, John. They're all poetic and well written."

"The word of God. What's in the bag?"

Esther plunked her load on the kitchen counter. "Dinner. I told you I'd make dinner for us tonight."

"You could have cooked it here."

"The cook at my house made this. I don't know much about cooking."

"My goodness, I better teach you something." Lucia stood her violin upright on the couch and gave her a pout. "You'll never hold onto a man without good cooking."

Before dessert, Lucia closed the windows and played another violin piece. After that she produced some toll house cookies from a jar and they relaxed on the couch. "Esther, I'm really proud of you. Sorry if I pushed you too fast. I couldn't help myself, but now that you've accepted Jesus, you've taken the first big step. Don't be discouraged if its only one baby step at a time until…"

"Until what?"

"Until you are tested, my dear."

"Uh oh. Something bad coming?"

"Not necessarily. All things work for good in His hands, but I have a sense there's a challenge coming for you soon. Does your mobster husband know you're seeing me?"

"Nah, don't worry. I only leave the place when I'm alone. He hasn't even called for weeks—probably thinks if he leaves me alone I'll calm down about the abortion."

"You've come a long way with the Lord, Esther. Perhaps the challenge for you will be to forgive Jimmy."

Esther checked out the ceiling and blew up her cheeks. "Whew, I know I should, huh? I'll try, but right now I just want to say thanks to you, Lucia. Don't know why you care about me but you've been my savior in more than one way."

"On the contrary, my dear, on this Earth *you* are the one who saved me. Even with faith to keep me going, I have to admit I was getting pretty lonely and despondent before you came along."

Esther frowned. "Oh, Lucia, I'd hate to think of you being sad. Is it just because you live alone? Don't worry, I'll always be around and if John's right, so will Jesus. It's in that chapter you gave me, fourteen, I think."

"Wow." Lucia shook her head. "Fourteen eighteen. You're a lot smarter than you look, aren't you?"

"I liked it 'cause He said we wouldn't be orphans anymore." She searched the living room. "Haven't seen Sassy tonight. Is she at the neighbor's?"

"Uh uh, pet door's closed." Lucia chuckled. "She'll be upstairs in my bedroom closet. Cats aren't violin fans you know. Hey, you ready for that cooking lesson?"

GOOD NEWS

You did not choose me

But I chose you and appointed you

To go and bear fruit—fruit that will last.

Jn 15: 16

Esther walked along the outer edge of the sidewalk then ducked into the space between the neighbor's Italian Cypress trees and the wall surrounding her house. She had hidden a wooden crate behind a bush and used it to jump high enough to get her arms over the top of the wall. *Good. No gardener around and no cars in the driveway.*

She pulled herself up with a grunt, dropped down onto her grounds below and took another look around. *All clear.* She sprinted to a live oak tree near the house and climbed it branch to branch.

Now, here's the tricky part. Esther jumped to her open second story bathroom window getting her arms over the sill. Her knees crunched against the stucco wall. *Ouch.*

Once inside she pulled up her jeans, cleaned a bleeding scrape, and applied a Band Aid. She freshened up, went downstairs and found Ginny, a panicked look on her face.

"Este, they must know. I heard cook talk to mister Izzy. I think they know you leave. They not happy."

"Well, I'm a lot happier. No big deal Gin. If it were, I think Jimmy would show up and cuss me out."

"Really? But is good to see you happy again. Tell me how you getting away, and about Miss Lucia."

"I've been sneaking off the grounds for months now, Ginny. There's a spot in the side yard where the front and back cameras don't see. I simply slip out the second floor bathroom window, hop onto a branch and go down the Live Oak. From there I use the gardener's ladder to go over the wall into the neighbor's place. I just got back."

"Oh that simple, huh?" Ginny laughed. "But why Lucia make you happy?"

Esther plumped down on a couch and patted the seat next to her, "Unhand that vacuum, young woman, and sit with me."

"I get you coffee or some thing?"

"No, no. Just sit with me." She patted the cushion again.

Ginny sat down slowly with a grin. "We just being friends now?"

That made Esther laugh. "Gin, we are *always* friends. And as you know, before I met Lucia you were my *only* friend. She's been like the grandmother I never had. We talk about, well *everything*, and she has such wise advice, too. We've become really close, but here's *my* advice: if you meet her don't accept her invitation to play Scrabble."

"Ah, it is talking make you happy? I sorry I not talk too good."

Esther picked up her hand and held it in both of hers. "Don't be silly. I love you just the way you are, and don't we still sneak away for lunches and time in the park when we can? No, the happiness part comes from the truth about God. Lucia led me to the point where I could pray and ask God to show me if he was real."

"I think there is God."

"I know you do, Ginny, but I haven't talked about this with you until I was sure about things myself. Last week I became really sure 'cause I felt the Lord come into my room when I was praying. He *showed* me He's real and He loves me--you too."

Esther patted her knee and made eye contact. "I know this will sound strange, but I feel God's inside of me now. I have a calmness, like I know I'll never be alone again. Lucia calls it being saved or born again in Christ."

"So she save you?"

"God does His own saving, but Lucia said I was the one who saved her in another way. She said I brought happiness back into her life. And Lucia taught me how wonderful it is to forgive people and pray for them."

"You forgive Jimmy?"

Esther sighed. "I'm still working on that one, Gin. I'll get there, but I did forgive my mother for leaving me."

"Can--can you tell me how I find the inside God and be safe too?"

"Sure can. And Ginny, it's not just being saved, but it's a call to action. Lucia told me that service for the Lord begins at the edge of your comfort zone. I've always been sort of shy, but I'm beginning to feel that telling people all about Him is exactly what I'm *supposed* to be doing with my life."

JIMMY

James Braugh looked down on the lights of The Vegas Strip from his casino corner office. He tried to decide which of two chorus girls would keep him company tonight. He decided he'd take both of them when his private phone rang. "Yeah, who's this?"

"Izzy, boss. This line secure?"

"Depends where *you're* calling from."

"I'm at Conklin's. It's about your wife."

"Yeah, what about her?"

"You gonna divorce her or what?"

"Haven't decided, but I don't want any bad press. What, she's been acting up again?"

"Yup, she's been wandering around. Real sneaky about it too. She turns off your system but a security camera at Sergio's across the street made her walking off a couple of times."

"She knows the car has a tracker but she could drive to the mall. Why's she do'in that?"

"I think she's still mad—maybe talking to people--maybe planning something."

"You spot where she goes?"

"No, but it's not good. Maybe it's accident time."

Jimmy chuckled. "Sure, that's how you get your jollies isn't it? Sorry but this has to be different cause she's my wife. First find out where she's going. Don't worry, I'll replace her real soon, but first I have to think of something."

"How about some drunk nails her when she crosses the street?"

Jimmy blubbered his lips. "Nah, she's just a kid and don't know better. But say, I have some fun for you after all. You know that scum bag running San Bernardino? He's been cooking the books."

"No kidding? Time for the other Captains to get a loyalty lesson, huh?"

"Hey!"

"Hey, what?"

"Hey, I just thought of something. Get Conklin up here four o'clock tomorrow, Sidney too. I just thought of how we'll give my wife a going away present and she's gonna do us a big favor too."

"Really?"

"Yeah, really. First get her a nice new thirty eight, a legal one, and register it in her name. Take her to the range and make sure she can shoot it."

"Right. Make like she shot at a 'burglar' huh?"

Jimmy laughed. "Stop salivating, Izzy. You watch too many movies. You're not gonna to shoot her, but still, you'll like the idea I just got. Tomorrow I'll show you how we're gonna solve *both* our problems with one stone, like they say."

PART TWO

NEAR SAN DIEGO, CA.

TWO YEARS LATER

LOST

I read once that "If a single man wins a fortune, he's soon to be married." so why do I feel like avoiding women and giving away every cent I own? William Mason sat at a corner table in the company break room, head drooped over a Styrofoam cup, and staring into his coffee.

Bill's long-sleeved royal blue shirt had a medium starch and he wore a tie—a bit formal for every day in Southern California. With a pout, he leaned his head on one hand and began to twist a curl of black, neatly gelled hair between his fingers. *Yeah, rejected as a husband by my wife and rejected as teacher by my school. So what good's the cash? If mom were alive, she'd give most of it to charity, and Dad? If I knew where he was, he'd say put it all on Trixie in the Eighth. Hey, maybe I will.*

In his peripheral vision Bill became aware of an approaching salmon-colored form weaving around the tables and maneuvering toward him with determination. He flashed an upward glance as a large woman smoothed the sides of her business suit, and eased into the chair opposite him. She cleared her throat, but he ignored her and kept his gaze fixed on the little white cup. He tilted his head slightly from one side to the other and began to twirl a coffee stirrer in his drink.

"William…" Her voice was barely perceptible. He flicked his head up at her and back down. "William, the *usual* thing I'd expect from a man who just inherited three hundred thousand dollars would be wild dancing in the street, showing off in a new car, and at least one of our pretty receptionists clinging to your arm."

Bill reluctantly accepted eye contact. "How'd you—oh, I remember, you're that HR person. The Estate lawyer found me when he contacted you."

She relaxed her arms on the table and sighed. "Yes, William, but I'm also our company's counselor. You've only been with us five weeks. Your work has been fine, superb really. I'm just concerned that you haven't made any friends, and you seem depressed. Are you?"

Bill leaned back and scowled. "So this little chat is because your job here at Perga Systems is to check up on the new guys, huh?"

Myrna exhaled abruptly. "No, well not *really.* I'm just the type that worries about people. She folded her hands on the table and spoke in her soft voice again. Are you having thoughts of suicide, William?" He smirked and gave a quick snort. "There, I *thought* so."

Bill squinted at her for a second then dropped his gaze to the silver dove pinned to her lapel. He found it strangely fascinating. "I've noticed what you do around here. Myrna, isn't it?" She nodded. "And I've also heard you're our official company Mother Hen."

Myrna chuckled and looked up at the ceiling. Her eyes sparkled. "Mother *Hen.* I like that. I suppose I am. And you'll find out how persistent mother hens can be, too. You might as well tell me why you're depressed, or I'll wring it out of you gradually. Let's see, you came to us from the East-- Hartford, I think. You were an instructor in computer science, right?"

Bill frowned. "Look, for your information, I am *not* suicidal, but I get the feeling I should be walking away right now."

"Of course you can, but please don't. I assure you this is *not* something for the company, and I won't put anything in your record. I really just want to help if I can."

"Well, you *can't,* but if you promise to leave me alone, I'll tell you."

Two Girl Scout fingers went up. "I promise."

"Okay, deal. I'm really a teacher, a High School teacher, and right now I should be teaching science and writing and English. It's what I'm *good* at. It's what I really *want* to be doing, but a lot of us got laid off." He sighed. "Hard times. Couldn't find a job."

"But you had a different job."

"Yeah, part-time sub for someone who was sick at the community college. You saw my application. That didn't last. My second love is writing novels. Got one published too. I thought I could live off the royalties."

"You get royalties?"

"Oh sure, enough to buy my lunch every day."

Myrna grinned. "Well, free lunches aren't bad."

He was back to coffee stirring and staring.

"I understand, William. You think the very things you love most in life are gone forever."

"And please stop calling me William. Bill is fine. But before you *probe* it out of me, and I can tell you *will*, I was only married once for six months. When I was laid off two years ago my wife divorced me and married a *stockbroker*. He used to be a good friend of mine too." The stirrer zinged across the table.

They sat quietly for an entire minute before Bill looked up at her with a sagging face. But the compassionate searching in Myrna's expression was so profound he jerked back as though he'd been slapped.

She shook her head. "I know. I know you wouldn't think you should listen to me. I'm one of the lucky ones, Bill. I love my job and I have a husband who adores chubby old me and our three teenagers. So maybe you think I can't relate, but I can."

Bill looked up and gave a little hand wave. "Sure, sure. Well, now I've told you. Thanks for the sympathy ma'am. Look, I gotta get back to work. Remember, you promised to leave me alone now, okay?"

Myrna skidded her chair back and got up. "That's true Bill. And a promise is a promise."

Bill was puzzled by the feeling he didn't want her to leave. She moved toward the door, but turned back, a mischievous glint now in her eye. "But come by my office at lunchtime if you're interested in an after hours *teaching* job I have for you."

"Huh?"

"You'd be teaching creative writing."

"Really?"

Yes, and by way, your students are all women." She winked.

Two men at the next table snickered.

THE PRICE

Consider that our present sufferings are not worth comparing with the glory that will be revealed in us. Rom. 8: 18

Esther shuffled along with her friend Nancy as they followed the line of green clad inmates down the corridor toward the prison's exercise yard. "Are you signing up for the writing course, Nance?"

Nancy tossed a hand in the air. "I dunno. I'm not much of a writer and they said that offering the course isn't final yet."

"But that's the point, my dear. Composition is part of the GED. You'll need that before you get out of here." She linked arms with her. "I'm not signing up if you don't."

"Yeah, well okay. I guess I will."

"Oh goodie." Esther did a little bouncy jump. "It'll be fun. You'll see."

"Hey, Esther, I just remembered. I'm supposed to be handing out water bottles outside." She pulled the work order out of her pocket to show the guard. "See you in the yard."

Nancy slipped out of line and jogged to the front. Esther sighed and resumed her forward shuffle. She glanced around at the nearby inmates. There was no one she knew, but she spoke up anyway. "This is boring, huh guys? How about we sing something cheerful? It's allowed if we all do it together, right?"

She faced forward, raised a hand as a pretend conductor, and began to sing. "Jesus loves me this I know, for the Bible tells me so. Yes, Jesus loves me. Yes…"

The blow to her delicate cheek bone came from behind and sounded like a hammer smashing into a melon. Esther silently fluttered downward like a large green leaf toward the concrete floor and lay unconscious.

The inmates stepped over and around her limp form. One laughed and gave her a kick. A heavy-set black woman bent down, grabbed her collar and slid Esther's body to the wall. When she propped her up she groaned and her eyelids began to flutter.

The woman studied the delicate face and frowned. "Hey girl, you're not dead yet. I'm Moneshia. Your head got pretty busted up. You awake?"

Esther slowly raised a hand to her face. She responded in a weak voice. "Hurts."

"Yeah, you all puffin up there."

A guard had come over and stood next to them contemplating the situation with a silent scowl. Moneshia looked up at her. "I'm gonna carry this baby to the Infirmary, okay?"

The guard shrugged. "Sure," and walked away.

Esther struggled to sit up on her own, coughed and grasped her helper's arm. "Just wait a sec—you said your name's Moneshia? Give me a minute." She looked up and squinted. "Things look a little fuzzy. I got hit, huh?"

"We should get you some aspirin or something."

Esther tried to smile. "That would make it bleed more, but it was kind of you to stop and help. Thank you."

"You got wacked all right, but you're just a little thing. I can carry you easy."

"Hold that thought. You might yet, but I'm going to try to stand up."

With her help Esther got up, swaying, but she stood upright. "Whew, my head really hurts. Guess I'm not going to faint though. I'm Esther, by the way."

The guard prodded a few curious stragglers to move on. Moneshia pouted. "What do you want me to do for you, little girl?"

"Looks like most everyone's already gone into the yard. Could you walk me out there and sing along with me? That'll help the pain a lot."

"Sure, whatever. But wait, you're lookin' like *this* and you still want to go out there?"

"You're beautiful, Moneshia."

She chuckled. "I get it. They knocked you down but you're just a givin' it right *back,* ain't cha? I don't know about your cause, but I gotta respect that. Let's go get em."

They passed the name-checker at the door. "You may have to keep holding me up, Moneshia. Do you know 'Nothing But The Blood'?"

She grinned. "My Momma couldn't cook us dinner without singing, and that one was maybe her favorite."

"Okay, I'll sing the first line and you the second."

"Sure." Still grinning, she nodded her head. "Course you *know* the guards will grab us in thirty seconds. Yeah and you don't care, right?"

Esther giggled. Fragile and bruised, the white girl and the hefty black woman walked out arm in arm into the sunlight to join the others. Nancy stood, hand over mouth, aghast at Esther's appearance when she passed by.

Esther began as loudly as she could, "What can wash away my sin?"

Moneshia laughed. She followed with concert hall resonance: "Nothing but the blood of Jesus."

"What can make me whole again?"

"Nothing but the blood of Jesus." Two guards began sprinting across the yard and that made Moneshia laugh again.

The guards grabbed the two singers and pulled them toward the exit, still singing at the top of their lungs. "Oh, precious is the flow--that makes me white as snow..."

Nancy stood crying at her water stand, one arm raised high, holding a bottle in her hand like the Statue of Liberty. She croaked, "You go, girl."

The hushed inmates could still hear the muffled song as the pair were pushed back inside the building. There was applause.

Nancy gave a hoarse shout. "Praise Jesus!"

OPPORTUNITY

Bill hesitated at the mahogany door, knuckles in knock-ready position. *She has to be up to some scheme. This could be a loyalty test or something, but she sure does that "I'm concerned about you" look so well.* He placed two delicate raps below the plastic "Human Resources" sign.

"Come right in," chimed the voice from within. Bill poked his head around. "Never need to knock on *this* door, Bill."

"You asked me to come by, Mrs. Simms?"

Myrna laughed and stood up. "First you want to be called Bill, but now I'm Mrs. Simms?" She gestured to a chair beside her desk, moved a pile of papers sitting between them, and faced him. "Sit, sit."

Bill gave a nervous cough and sat. "Look, I appreciate what you're trying to do for me, but…"

"For you? Nonsense. You'll be fine. I'm more interested in some others who really need our help." She pointed to a pitcher and a plate beside it on the edge of her desk and popped a round morsel from the dish into her mouth. “Ice tea and cheese balls—a little appetizer I made myself. Have some.”

Bill couldn’t think of anything to say so he poured a glass, took a sip and settled for giving her a “what-the-heck-is-going-on” look.

Myrna sat down but leaned forward to make unavoidable face to face contact. His eyes widened.

She spoke with her mouth full of food. “So, I bet you’re thinking we’re going to talk about your job, huh?” She swallowed. “Not at all. You’re a gifted young man and you’re probably bored with your evenings, right?”

Not to mention bored with this job and the town the evenings are in. “I’m fine with what I do at home, Myrna, and I’m not the least bit interested in being fixed up with a date if that’s on your mind.”

She leaned back with a grin and a chuckle. “Oh I hardly think you need any *fixing up*, Bill. Try a cheese ball. I’ll feel hurt if you don’t.”

Bill took a cautious bite and studied her round, slightly ruddy face. *Okay, I’m done guessing, lady. Not a word until you come out with it.*

Myrna sighed and glanced at the ceiling. “Hang on a sec. I forgot to get this file out for you. Most people think I’m organized, so don’t tell on me.”

While she began rummaging through her desk file drawer, Bill’s gaze wandered about the room. The wall shelves were cluttered with books in sloppy order, travel souvenirs, and children’s toys. A picture on the far wall showed kids crowded around some man wearing a white toga and the inscription “God is Love”. *Maybe this woman is a little nuts.*

On her desk, a “family at the beach” photo seemed to be staring at him. The joy-filled, laughing people appeared as though they were about to leap out of the frame and happily dance over the desk in front of him. Bill had to turn away.

“Ah, here it is. There’s a request for a writing instructor: should be just a half dozen students or so. They’re not far from here and the request is for one hour sessions every Thursday at seven. Interested in teaching them?”

“Usually schools recruit tutors from their own staff. Is it a high school? What’s it pay?”

Myrna chuckled and tilted her head. “No pay at all, mister, at least not cash. But you’d be building your resume and helping people in need. It’s at the women’s State Penitentiary.”

Bill threw his head up, slid his chair back and stood up. "Okay, I think we're done here."

Myrna sprang up. "Oh no, wait, Bill. Please don't be hasty. You'd be back to the teaching you love and these people really need your help."

"You expect me to sit in a room with a bunch of convicts? And how come you even know about their so-called need?"

"I volunteer for Kairos. It's a Christian prison ministry. We go there to deliver the message of Jesus. We also deliver cookies and good cheer."

Bill threw out his arms. "Oh right, so now you want me to be a *minister*, huh? I don't even like that spiritual stuff."

Myrna leveled her gaze, her tone soft but clear. "William Mason, there are people out there calling for your help as a *teacher* not a minister. No one expects you to even mention Christianity in class, and they'd ding you if you did."

She sat down slowly and took on a hungry puppy dog expression. "Please don't think I'm high pressuring you. It's okay to say no, really it is. But these women are getting their GED and want a better education so they can have a life after prison." Her brows lowered. "But Bill, on a personal note if I may be so bold, I do think you need to be needed right now."

Bill turned away and took a few brisk steps to the door, but paused. He leaned on the door frame with an outstretched arm and studied the floor in a moment of silence. He coughed. "Any chance they might need a science teacher, too?"

THE BIG HOUSE

It was six-thirty in the evening when Bill pulled into a nearly empty visitor's lot. The windowless concrete wall near him stretched way out in both directions. *Why am I nervous? I sailed through the volunteer training they gave me. Remember, there's just a classroom and students in there.*

Briefcase swinging from one arm, Bill went up the steps at a brisk pace and went through an open wrought iron gate. An arrow sign marked "Employees" directed him to the left where he was greeted by a well guarded booth. A male guard patted him down and inspected his driver's license and letter of invitation.

The officer had him complete a short form and buzzed him through a door and into the building where he faced another security check point. *Good grief. They'll undress me next.*

The next guard was a slim woman, blonde hair bound in a short pony tail and straight, thin lips. "Please empty your case out on this table, sir." She slid his wood ruler, pencils, phone and laptop aside. "You can keep the books and writing pad, but chalk and short pencils will be provided in the classroom." She gave him a badge to wear and he received his first smile. "Have a good day, Mr. Mason."

That felt better. "Thank you. You too."

Bill turned to go in but to his surprise he was confronted by a tall black man sporting a big grin and a Hawaiian shirt.

"Hi, I'm Jim Givens. On behalf of Kairos and Claremont State Prison, welcome."

"You know Myrna? She talked me into this. I'm just here on a one day trial, you know."

Jim nodded. "I guess most everyone around here knows our lady of action. She asked me to meet you for a brief orientation."

Jim ushered him around a corner past a sign reading "Yard B". The tan painted concrete block walls had a unique aroma that reminded him of high school.

"Okay Mr. Mason, basically you're only allowed books, and papers. No electronics. That's why they took your stuff, but you can pick up your gear when you leave. There's a fixed computer in the classroom and it's okay to bring a flash drive but they'll take it in for you.

"So guns and hack saws are out then?"

"There will be at least one guard with you at all times and anything you wish to give the students goes to her first."

"So no files either?"

Jim grinned. "Just the paper kind."

They reached a point in the corridor where iron bars blocked entry, and Jim shook his hand. "All right, show your pass through the bars to this guard. I'll be leaving you, but remember the inmates really do appreciate what you're doing. Some might not know how to say it, but they really do. Thanks for volunteering and God bless."

Bill returned a pained smile and held out his badge for the next guard. "Sure, Jim, but will I ever see the outside again?" Jim chuckled, and walked away with a quick wave.

Bill's gaze fixed on the dark eyes and lowered brows of this inner guard. She was a Hispanic woman, not quite as tall as he was, but she clearly outweighed him. She checked his badge and slid the steel door aside with a loud clink. "I'll take you to your classroom Mr. Mason."

They started down a corridor with high, narrow windows and the sound of conversations outside. The door clanged shut behind them. Bill cringed. He dropped a book and fell on his knees to get it.

The guard laughed and helped pull him back up. "I'm officer Diaz. Never been in a prison before, have you?"

"I, no, uh. I'm fine. Thank you."

The tough lady had transformed into a woman with motherly understanding. "Nothing to worry about, Mr. Mason. The inmates you'll meet are the ones who are really interested in getting ahead, and unlike high school, if anyone misbehaves I'll be there to clunk em on the head."

Bill grinned. "Well that's good, but they could get their GED online. Why the interest in a live teacher?"

Diaz paused at the classroom door and squinted at him. "You think a computer teaches better than you do?" He shook his head. "Didn't think so. Besides, there's no internet allowed anyway, and they like meeting folks from the outside."

She opened the door and the familiar sound of laughing and chatting students resonated in the concrete, windowless room. *Smells like a basement in here.* He slid behind the desk with his briefcase. Diaz shouted. "Hey! Knock it off, people. Teacher's here. Take your seats."

The guard moved back to the door and sat on a stool. Suddenly, there was complete silence, an awkward, expectant quiet. Seven students sat in their desk-chairs, studying the strange creature who stood before them. Bill gulped. He felt awash in a sea of green.

Bill Mason introduced himself to his monochromatic students, got up and turned to write his name on the blackboard. *Oh yes, snickering behind my back—beginning to feel like home.*

He pulled out a clipboard from his case, walked around and sat on the front of his desk only a few feet from the front row. The guard gave him a worried look. "Okay, normally I'd start with some lame joke, and I was ready to say 'I didn't know I was in Orange County'. But here you are all in *green*, so the joke's on me."

He faced expressionless stares. *At least the guard seemed to enjoy that.*

"First, I'm supposed to take attendance, but we're a small class and I want to get to know each of you." He gestured to his left. "Starting with the front row, tell us your full name, what type of writing you are doing, if any, or at least what type of writing you'd like to learn."

He nodded at a scowling black woman. "Ms?"

"Uh…" She dropped her head, eyes fixed on the floor. "Moneshia Washington. I like to learn how to write a kick-ass letter to a good lawyer. Maybe I can get a retrial."

Murmuring chuckles. Someone said "Good luck with *that*, Mo."

He flashed a finger-point at her. "Letter writing skills—very important. We'll work on them."

Bill turned his gaze toward the next woman whose dark eyes were fixed on him. "Alverez. Getting out in six months. My uncle says he can get me a job at his plant writing instructions and stuff, but I need a GED."

"You have a first name Ms. Alvarez?"

"Maria, but we go by last ones in here."

"In this classroom we're on a fist name basis, Maria."

Next was a tight-lipped middle-aged woman with a leathery tan and mousey hair bound up in a tight bun. "Judy Pyle. Just need a GED." She shrugged. She'd said her piece.

"Any type of writing interest you, Judy?"

"Maybe."

"How about reading—what do you like to read?"

"Cycle mags."

Bill shrugged. "Maybe after this class you'll be writing articles for them." He pointed to the last one in front, a round faced woman and the only one with a smile. She had teased out her short red hair so it flipped out. "Prisoner 1628, present. Moved here 'cause they said So Cal is so 'captivating'. Never knew they meant I'd be a *captive*. Writing about the funny side of this here tank life. Might even have a book going." She crossed her eyes.

Bill grinned. "Well good. You have a name too?"

"Oh my *outside* name? Mary, quite contrary, Stearns."

He chuckled. "I'm smiling already, Mary."

Moving to the three in the back row, he pointed to the woman on the end. She had delicate features, light complexion and fine, flax colored hair. This contrasted sharply with a swollen purple bruise that partly closed her right eye, but her left eye twinkled brightly. She offered a broad grin. "Prisoner 1171 here."

"Looks like you were bitten by the cell door, huh?" The other inmates responded with loud laughter. One turned and threw a spitball. The woman next to her reached out and slapped away the incoming missile. *Uh oh, didn't see that coming.*

Diaz rushed over and faced the class. "Hey! What do you think this is, fifth grade? The next one who does something stupid is *out* of the class. You hear?"

Bill spoke softly to the bruised woman. "I'm sorry, Ms., my remark was rude." The guard returned to her stool but kept her scowl with a raised finger. "Go on Ms., your name?"

1171 kept her unperturbed grin. "Oh, clumsy me." Her voice sounded pure, almost child-like. "My name is Esther Green…"

"But now she's Esther *blue*," Alverez guffawed. Some laughed.

"Esther Green, and I want to write children's stories and illustrate them with drawings." More chuckling.

Alverez pretended to throw something and Diaz shouted: "Hey!" She spread open her hands and flashed an innocent look at Diaz.

"Esther, that's great. Children's stories are more difficult than you'd think, though. I'll show you how word choice and the voice you choose are important." He pointed to the olive complected woman beside her who had deflected the spitball.

"Ngami Bhutto, but my friends call me Nancy. I have an idea for a murder mystery."

"Super, Nancy. And finally," He pointed to the last one, a black woman with straightened black hair and a sneer.

"I'm writing a documentary on police brutality." She glanced at the guard. "And maybe *guard* brutality."

"Documentaries are good. They require research, though. Your name?"

"I'm livin' the research, mister. Name's Oprah Winfrey." Laughter broke out.

"Come on now."

"Yeah well, it's Ophelia, though. Really. Ophelia Scarlett, and folks call me Oprah."

Bill stood up and swung around and went back to sit behind his desk. "Well, that was a fun start. I really hope everyone will enjoy this class and maybe even learn something. This isn't a class in English grammar, but I'll go over any errors that come up. First, any questions?"

Maria raised her hand. "Mr. Mason, could you give me some private lessons in my room later?"

Raucous laughter. The guard strode out in front and gave them another quick lecture on expulsion rules. When she turned away Alvarez gave her "the finger".

A hand was waving. "Mary Stearns? A real question I hope, and no jokes."

"Yeah. How you gonna give us grades?"

Bill nodded. "A good question. Your final grade will depend on how much you've improved. This will partly be a creative writing class, so even if you can't compose a decent sentence now, but by the end the course if you're creative and coherent, you'll get an A."

"But what if I'm already writing like a pro?"

Bill chuckled. "Well then maybe you don't need to be here. But if you're an unchanged Hemingway from start to finish, you'd probably get a C plus." He reached into his brief case and brought out a little stack of books. "Here, you each get one of these."

Diaz, the guard hastened over before he could get up and approach the students. She began to hand them out for Bill who added, "These are pocket dictionaries with basic grammar guides courtesy of the Kairos Mission."

Ngami waved her hand.

"Yes?"

"This doesn't take the place of their cookies, does it?"

"I'm sure you'll still get those, Nancy."

The next half hour was spent teaching basic composition and sentence structure. Then Bill announced: "Okay, class. Your homework assignment is…"

Red hair began to bounce. "Oh goodie. We really get to go *home* then?"

Bill laughed. "You know what I mean, Miss Contrary. I want each of you to write two pages on whatever interests you." He lowered his eyebrows at Judy. "You can write a pretend article for Cycle Magazine if you want. But don't copy something. I'll know."

"All right, we have about twenty minutes left so right now I want each of you to put your name on top of a blank sheet and write a paragraph or two on the same subject." He looked up at the ceiling. "Let's see—the subject is a bird on a branch."

Maria was shaking her head. "You're kidding, right?"

"Nope, dead serious. Whatever comes to mind, but a bird and a branch have to be in it. Be creative. No grades here; just have fun with it. I'll look over what you've written after class, and we'll discuss them next week."

THE BOSS

Isadore Croft oozed through the dimly lit evening crowd at Bennie's Vegas Bar, music booming, pole dancers slinking, slot machines clinking. The air was heavy with smoke, perfume and perspiration. He nodded at the waitresses he passed by, patting two of his favorites on their behinds as he worked his way to the door in the back.

The passkey dangling from his neck let him in the first door but he paused and took in a deep breath when he reached the relative quiet inside. He ran a comb through his sleek black hair and buttoned his shiny green jacket. Climbing the stairs to his right he came to a thick mahogany door at the top. Isadore didn't knock, but touched a small button high on the door jam and waited half minute until the door opened on its own. He took two steps inside stopped and coughed.

A large-framed man sat behind a massive desk looking at a monitor and smoking a cigar. Still looking at his monitor, he gave a flick of his hand motioning that he could now be approached. "Whatcha got for me Izzy?"

"Mostly good reports today, Mr. Conklin. Our two little Denver ladies were delivered safely to the buyers in Chiapas. Cash all wired in. The Colombian coke came in to Tucson last night. It's already split up and sent on to our Captains. No sign of Sherlock on our trail this time."

A massive blue-black cloud rose from his mouth. "Commissions sent out to those who worked the deals?"

"Absolutely."

"So what about the 'mostly'?"

"Oh, that. Well, you said you didn't care if that 'Green woman' stirred up trouble in the pen, but now she's signed up for a writing course. She's face to face with an outsider, maybe start talking."

Conklin put down his smoke and leveled his gaze on Izzy. "Someone watching her?"

"Yeah, Alvarez. She's signed in the class with her."

"Good. I'm not worried just yet. Let me know what she reports."

Izzy tossed a glance to the ceiling. "You know I *told* Jimmy he should a had her disappear when the time came."

Conklin's wide face frowned. He stared at Izzy for a moment, his head bobbing slightly. "Didn't anyone teach you common decency? She was his wife."

"Trophy wife, and she isn't anymore. Jimmy's gone but she knows too much, especially about me."

"She did us a service, Izzy."

"Not exactly a volunteer though, huh?"

Conklin threw his head back with a deep throaty laugh. "You're right there, but listen: she's harmless at the moment so leave her alone. Just let me know if 'Miss Goody-Two-Shoes' starts yapping to anyone on the outside, I mean *besides* the classroom where Alverez is watching her."

NEXT WEEK

Bill was early for his class and sat at the desk organizing papers as the students began to shuffle in. Esther had acquired a limp and clearly her nose appeared to be broken.

"Good evening, everyone. Please sit where you were last week so I can remember who you are.

Diaz, the guard, came in behind them, went over to Bill's desk and spoke softly. "I warned them about outbursts, Mr. Mason. Should be quieter this time." She handed him a pile of papers. "Here's their homework."

Bill looked over the group and winced when he focused in on Esther's face. Her broken nose was tilted to one side. He turned to the guard who was heading for her corner. "Ms. Diaz what…" *Better not say anything. Remember last time?* Diaz didn't turn around anyway.

Esther saw his anguished concern as he looked at her. She mouthed the words, "It's okay."

Bill bit his lip and mouthed back, "No, it's not." He forced a big smile. "Welcome back class. I can see everyone's here, and thank you for your homework."

He picked up some typed papers and pulled his chair around to the front of the desk. "I don't like hollering from back there. It's easier to talk to you close up." Scattered tittering. Diaz rolled her eyes up at the ceiling.

"First off, I want to say that you ladies have surprised me. All of you are already writing at least close to high school level and two of you are closet professionals."

Mary said, "I can tell you who's the *professional.*" They laughed.

"Now ladies, you know what I really mean. I shouldn't have been surprised. You're seven out of over four hundred who volunteered for this writing course.

"I typed out your ten minute "bird and branch" compositions and I have copies for each of you so you can see what your classmates are writing."

Mary waved her hand, this time to be recognized. "But they're anonymous, aren't they, Mr. Mason?"

"Not at all, Mary. I don't care what goes on in the rest of this 'funny can' as you call it, but in *here,* this is our special club. Everyone helps and shares as equals."

The inmates glanced around at one another. Bill waited while the puzzled looks mostly faded into demure smiles, even Alvarez. "Okay, I also notice that each of you are so creative that no two themes you came up with are even *remotely* similar. Moneshia writes about 'jail birds' and what branch of government to write to if you're treated unfairly."

"Now Maria Alvarez…" he looked into her eyes as she struggled for a defiant look, "she wrote a piece about a hawk on a branch searching for prey and swooping down to catch and tear them apart." He chuckled. "A little gruesome in the details, but well written." She grinned.

"And then there's our Ms. 'I just want a GED'." He grinned at Judy. You've surprised me most of all. I hope it won't embarrass you, but I'm going to read your piece aloud." Bill took a breath and glanced around until he was sure his audience was attentive.

> "Old Jim feathered the throttle. His aging cycle alternately roared and sputtered along the highway. *I could pull over and try advancing the spark. Nah, this bird just needs new plugs and I got more important things to tend to.*

He patted the wings on the gas tank in front of him. *Come on, Old Bird. You'll make it.*

Jim peeled off on the branch road and headed up a winding path into the mountains. It had been five years since the incident at 'The Stagecoach Bar'. Maybe she wouldn't even be there anymore. Dangerous, he knew, but he was going anyway. *Doesn't matter what happens to me now. It's time."*

"Alright folks, that's what the first few lines of a good novel look like. I really want to know all about old Jim, his cycle, what happened before and what will happen next. Why doesn't it matter? Can't you just taste it?" He nodded at Judy. "Well done." He gave her a quick salute. She couldn't conceal an evanescent smile.

Bill leaned back in his seat and nodded. "Now don't misunderstand; most everyone has made some errors, Judy too. We have plenty to work on, but you guys are all creative, each in your own way.

Bill chuckled. "I wasn't going to read Mary's, but I'm sorry. Now I can't resist. You might guess she's in my science class too."

He gave her a tilted head shake and a tight-lipped smile that said: "You're naughty". "So here it is."

> The world's first bird, a giant pterodactyl, sat on a branch. He was looking at some pretty annoying stuff below. "Ah, there's one of those mammals. I heard them say they would rule the world."
>
> "Really?" So he swooped down and ate em up.
>
> Then he saw some time-traveling humans. "Yuch. Listen to *them.* Sounds like they'll *really* mess up the world big time."
>
> So he swooped down and ate em up too.

Through the laughter, Bill shook his head. "Comedian or prophet, I don't know which." Eyes to the ceiling, Mary grinned and shook her orange doo.

Bill swiveled his chair and pointed to the first one on the back row. "All right shake that off if you can and get ready for a complete change of pace. Imagine yourself putting a young child to bed. This is a bed time story, a Christian one by Esther Green."

Maria coughed and said "I'll bet."

Moneshia gave her a swift elbow. "Cool it. Lay off her, ya'hear." Maria's look of shock faded into a nod that said "Okay."

Bill gave a little cough and straightened in his seat. "All right, here goes."

> "Baby bird landed on the branch with a painful thump. She'd fallen from the nest above. Who pushed her? She looked down.
>
> *Oh, my gosh. It's so far down and it's getting dark.*
>
> She huddled up against the trunk, shivering from the cold.
>
> *It's freezing out here and no one came with all my peeping.*
>
> She thought she would die but remembered what mother had said. "God even counts every sparrow and provides for them all."

The next morning, she woke in the sunshine. She felt warmer but very hungry. *Oh, there's that human child down below filling up the bird feeder, but it seems so far away and I don't know how to fly, do I?*

Grown up birds were eating at the feeder. *Gosh, there's nuts and seeds and even a piece of suet, but it's so far down. If I jump, I might die. But mother told us, "A leap of faith is always rewarded."*

She spread her wings, but they seemed so little. *Look at me. I'm too small to fly. But mother said,* "All God's creatures are wonderfully made, and can do as He intended."

She flapped a little and barely bounced off the branch. *I'm scared. But what else did mother say? "If you have faith, it will be the wind beneath your wings. You will soar like an eagle."*

> Baby bird gripped the branch with tiny feet and blinked up at the sky. *God, I do believe you made me, and I* *do* *have faith in you. If you made me to fly, be with me now.*
>
> Little bird leaped off the branch and flapped her wings. At first she just fell but then she spread her wings as far as they would go. Suddenly she felt she'd become an eagle indeed.
>
> Little girl bird soared to the feeder and landed with a splash in the seeds. She looked back up into the sky and said "Thank you, Lord".

Bill nodded toward Esther. "I'm impressed. I'll read that to my kids if I ever have any. Some of your word choices may be too adult, however."

"Nancy likes mysteries, remember? Here's her submission:"

> Ten PM Tuesday night. Vulture sat on his favorite branch by the lake. Fishermen leave fish remains there. Ten-twenty: a white dodge pickup bumps along the path by the lake. Two

> men get out dragging a tied up man. They shoot him, pull off his hood and untie his hands. Ten-twenty-five: They toss out a woman and drop a gun on her. Ten-thirty: They take off rubber gloves and drive off. Ten-thirty-five: Vulture thinks he'll peck at the corpses, but the woman moves. She's alive. Vulture waits. Vultures don't talk.

Bill tilted his head to one side with a pained smile. "Definitely *not* a good bedtime story, but we all want to know what happens next. It has staccato-like short sentence action. Very good, Nancy."

"And finally, Scarlett. Hers is…"

"Mr. Mason, stop." She had a stone faced frown. "You never said *everyone* would hear these. This is embarrassing."

Bill took a moment to soften his look and tone. "It's all right, Scarlett. All writing is okay in this room."

"But, I was just being silly."

"Silly can be fun. You can write serious stuff next time, so hang on."

> Girl bird hangin' on a branch lookin' for a boy bird.

Tweet, tweet, tweet.
"There's a guy bird in the next tree.
He's a lookin' too."
Sweet, sweet, sweet.
"Hey, now it's my way he's a lookin'.
This handsome guy
Makes my heart just break, break, break."
"Wow, he flew to my tree. Oh gosh, what a great couple we'd make, make, make."

"Now Oprah, don't look so upset. I like this too, and it's certainly not about police brutality, is it?"

Several laughed and someone said "That's just dumb."

Bill shook his head. "Oh yeah, you know what I see in this? Song lyrics. With a little polish and a consistent point of view, Ms. Scarlett might sell this to a Disney film."

Oprah was frowning up at the ceiling, one hand raised, but when she lowered her gaze on her teacher, her expression had turned into gratitude.

Bill returned to the blackboard. "All right ladies, before all of you get too overconfident we'll go over some errors in each piece. Everyone can learn something from someone else's mistakes. First thing next time we'll review the homework you brought. This week I want each of you to expand your bird and branch pieces to four hundred words or so, or if you prefer, write a different short story."

He gave them a little bow. "Great start, ladies."

NEXT MONTH

The ladies filed in, laughing and giggling. Judy's lips were pursed as she suppressed a smile, and even Alvarez had a grin. *Well, they are sure getting along better.* He spotted Mary with crossed eyes and a tongue showing. *Ah, there's their entertainer.*

Bill searched for Esther behind the crowd. She was smiling but her left arm was sporting a bandage so large it reminded him of Popeye. *This is killing me. Why would anyone want to hurt her?*

"Hi everyone. Thanks for mailing me your assignments. Today we're going to review these newspaper articles you sent in. Whether you write on line, or in print, you're developing a skill that can actually pay. So even if you really want to write poetry, here's a potential day job. Yes, Nancy?"

"But, how would you actually land a job like that?"

"Good question. The quick answer is to send an editor a sample of your work along with a great query letter like the one we worked on last week. If you have any interest or experience in something, by all means promote it. You know, like Judy and motorcycles."

He pulled out the folder of papers and grinned at his students. "Once again, I'm impressed with your creativity. On the theme of 'body found beside the road', no two approaches are the same. In one we have a corpse body holding a shotgun but riddled with bullets, another has the Mayor's wife as the victim, and another writes about a lone boy with no identification.

"Not surprisingly, Mary's body is a possum who gets up, bites the reporter on the leg, and runs off." He chuckled. "And Esther's was creative too."

Nancy gave her an elbow nudge but it jarred Esther's bandage and she winced in pain. Bill stopped himself from saying anything, but as compassion overwhelmed him, their eyes locked. She smiled a little and mouthed the words "It's okay."

He returned his gaze to the others. "Esther wrote about two little girls discovering a dead crow and giving it a ceremonial burial. If I ran a children's magazine, I'd buy it. Very cute."

"All right ladies, today you will each pick a number from one to seven and get a random article written by one of your fellow students. I want you to edit it with the red pencils Diaz is handing out. Make comments on it good or bad, and suggest changes. Editing is all important to a good writer, and part of your final exam will be similar. For that you'll all get a short story full of mistakes to correct."

Moneshia's hand shot up. "But what about the GED? Is this test easier?"

Bill grinned. "You guys will *crush* the GED, every one of you. Not to worry."

As the students began to work on the papers, Bill found his gaze once more locked with Esther's soft blue eyes."

ANOTHER MONTH LATER

The Lord knows how to rescue godly
Men from their trials. 2Pet. 2: 9

Myrna leaned on the corner of the cubicle wall and waited for him to stop typing. "Bill, I have the information you e-mailed me about."

Bill looked up. "Oh Myrna, thanks." He stood, smiled and gestured to his only other chair. "First, I want to thank you for hooking me up with teaching this group. It's really been fun and I've been surprised by the writing abilities of these students."

"Convicts can write?" Myrna teased.

He snorted. "Can they *ever*. They're about to graduate and no one will get less than a C+. What did you turn up on Judy Pyle?"

"Sorry, not much. She's never published anything; dropped out of high school after three years. *But,* other than math, she got straight A's. She managed to audit a college course on American Literature by impersonating a student who dropped out."

"So, she had an earlier conviction?"

"Nah, the Dean dropped the charges. For the last five years she's been with a motorcycle gang drifting around the country. The current record shows she was in a fight with another gang and she was convicted of assault. One witness said she hit a man who was shooting her boyfriend with a two by four, but she was too late."

"Ouch. That wasn't self defense?"

"The rival gang told another story."

"That's too bad. Judy doesn't say much, but she's a born novelist—probably doesn't even realize it. She has an amazing grasp of what makes a story really good. Descriptions just flow out of her. She's *way* better that I am, Myrna."

Myrna sat up with a wiggle and a grin. "Well, you just keep encouraging her. She probably read a lot in school, and she'll be getting out in four months. I'm told they have a job lined up for her. Guess what it is?"

"Freelance copywriter?"

"How about motorcycle mechanic."

He chuckled. "Not surprised, but I think I'll buy her a laptop for a discharge present, anonymous, of course."

"Anything else, Bill?"

"Yeah. You got time to talk?"

Myrna's eyebrows lowered. "Course."

"There's this one woman. I can't get her out of my mind."

He saw her expression and shook his head. "Oh, not what you're thinking, Myrna. It just that every week she has a new injury, and some of them are really *bad.* Makes me feel just awful. I want to do something to help her but I'm not sure what."

She nodded. "Unfortunately, that sort of thing's not rare. Don't bother telling the warden. She'll take some action, but that might actually make it worse for the woman."

"That's what I think, too. Oh Myrna, she's so sweet and delicate, though. I just can't *stand* it."

Myrna's expression reverted to her powerful compassion. "I—I'll make some discrete inquires, but I doubt I can help. What's her name?"

"Esther Green, and I'm going to visit her. That's allowed, isn't it?"

"Not allowed. Even though you're not paid, you are considered an employee and visiting is considered fraternization. Also she doesn't have to see you, you know."

"Couldn't I call it a faculty consultation?

"Nope. That would be in the classroom with a guard present."

"Well, I'll figure something out. I have to talk to her. Her face is keeping me up at night."

"Is your fall course about finished?"

"Myrna, you're right! After finals next week, I'll quit. You're a genius."

"Really? Why am I now feeling I just don't know when to stop talking?"

VISITING HOURS

The dark December clouds and cold, billowing rain reminded Bill of April in Connecticut. Inside the gate he had to turn the other way toward the visitor entrance instead of the employees. *This is really busy, a much bigger operation than on the employee side.*

Like the airlines queues, everyone emptied their pockets into baskets and went through detectors, but on this side they all crowded around a registration desk when they got through. There was paperwork and IDs, but finally everyone sat in the waiting room. *Wonder if she'll even see me. I should have given her some notice.*

A female guard entered and explained procedure. "Six at a time for those with cards marked booths, then another six in fifteen minutes. You'll go through the door on your right." She pointed to the other door. "The rest of you go to the open visitation room. We can take twelve people at a time."

After the first six left with another guard, she went behind the counter and called out: "Mister Donner, please come up to the desk."

She spoke to Donner just above a whisper, but his responses grew louder.

"Will you just go back and ask her? I'm trying to be nice here."

"I realize you've seen her before but she won't see you *today*."

"I know she blames me for what happened, but she *has* to see me, doesn't she? She's my wife."

"Sorry, sir, but she does not. No inmate can be forced to visit."

"Look, lady, I'm telling you: just go back in there and tell her to come out."

Now speaking firmly: "She won't see you now, but why don't you just write her"

Donner wacked the desk with his fist. "Bitch!" He stomped off, muttering.

Bill sighed and looked around at the others. *Most of them look tougher than the inmates I've seen.* Wait over. He was called in the next group, but stopped to ask the guard. "How come I can't see my inmate in the open seating?"

She glanced at his card. “She’s level four. Booths required.”

He shrugged his shoulders and was ushered into a wide corridor with six semi-private booths in a line. Each booth was shielded by thick glass from the room beyond and they sat him down in one.

Prisoners began to file in. *Don’t see her—oh there’s Esther in the doorway talking to that Diaz guard. She’s giving the guard a folder.*

Esther was dressed in a wrinkle-free tan shirt and a brown skirt. She glided over to him with a grin but she sported a Band-Aid that covered half her forehead. “Hi Bill. I can’t tell you how surprised and happy I am to see you. You’re my first visitor *ever*, you know.”

Diaz came around to Bill’s side and placed a spiral notebook in front of him. Esther continued. “That’s the sketchbook for my children stories. Please hold it for me in a safe place. They tore up my old one.” Esther looked up at him, her beautiful eyes wide with expectancy.

“I, uh—I thought I knew just what I wanted to say, but…” He shook his head. “You’re the strangest woman I’ve ever met.”

Esther giggled. “Oh please, no compliments. They go straight to my head.”

Bill grinned. "I'm sorry. I meant that to sound better. I'll look at these later if that's okay."

"Sure, and I like you too, Bill. So what's on your mind, 'mon professeur'?"

Bill let out a breath. "After all our weekly classes, I've gotten to know you and I care about you, Esther. But frankly I can't stand seeing you every week with a new injury. They look really painful, too. Isn't there something I can do about it?"

"You could try wearing dark glasses."

"Seriously, Esther, I want to help. Who's doing this to you?"

"Big Rita and her gang. She doesn't like me or what I'm doing, but there's nothing you can do to help. I am grateful you're concerned about me, though. I *really* am." She tilted her head and offered a weak smile.

"Couldn't I speak to the warden, or get you a lawyer?"

"That would make things worse, Bill, but I'm working on the situation my own way. I'm getting pretty good at karate avoidance moves. I got a book and I practice in my cell."

"I see a fresh Band-Aid."

"Ahh, just a scratch. I hit the wall dodging, but she missed me clean this time."

Bill shook his head and suppressed a smile. *I don't get it. She seems almost enthusiastic.* "But Esther, can you tell me why Rita, or anyone for that matter, could possibly want to harm you?"

"Sure." Her eyes brightened. "I've been talking about Jesus, and sixteen women have accepted Him as their Savior this past year. Two of them were in Rita's gang."

Bill lowered his brows in puzzlement. "Okay so you've been evangelizing. It's not my thing, but why should anyone care?"

"Big Rita is part of a Los Angeles mob and in here she practically runs Yard B. She feels threatened by my conversions since it is outside of her power. The worst was when those two women came to know the Lord just before they were released. They didn't return to the LA gang like they were supposed to and escaped into their new lives."

Bill puffed out his cheeks. "Okay, I get the situation. I don't like it, but I do understand."

"Don't worry, Bill. I feel the Lord has me here for a purpose."

"But how long will this last? You must be due for release soon. I can't imagine you doing anything illegal." A buzzer sounded. "What's that?"

"Two minute warning."

"Okay, I know it's not my right to ask, but I'll ask anyway. Would you tell me what you're in for, you know, the story of what happened?"

Esther laughed. "You're really sweet, you know. It's a long story, but I'll tell you on one condition. Of course you'll also have to come and visit me again."

"You just name it."

"Nothing painful. I want to pray a salvation prayer with you."

The back door opened and a guard entered behind the women. "That's all? Oh sure, Esther. I'll pray with you if that's what you want. Is our time up for today?"

All the women were standing up to leave but Bill shot one more question as Esther turned to go. "But just tell me what you're in for."

She turned her head back over her shoulder, bestowed an impish grin sprinkled with a wiggly-fingered goodbye gesture. "Murder one, Bill. I'm a lifer."

THE SAVIOR

God, our Savior wants all men to be saved and come to a knowledge of the truth. 1 Tim 2: 4

Next Saturday the visitor line for security was even longer and scented with a mixture of men's cologne, and what seemed like old gym socks. *Esther was so nonchalant when she walked away. Maybe she's just teasing me with that murder thing to pull my leg. But she's an artist, too, and a good one. Strange woman. Fascinating.*

Even though she was only thirty seconds late coming through the door, Bill had the anguished thought that she might not see him anymore. But finally, there she was, dressed in a green half-sleeve shirt and gliding smoothly to the window. She had no bruises or Band-Aids this time but her delicate nose retained a list to one side. "Hello, Bill. I hope you've been well."

The directness of her penetrating look made Bill feel she was etching words on the back of his skull. "Oh fine, and

I'm glad to see your face is recovering. First I want to compliment you on your illustrations. They're just perfect for a children's story. Professional quality."

That brought a smile. "Why thank you, Bill. Did you see I added a picture for the little bird on a branch?"

He chuckled and nodded.

She narrowed her eyes and spoke directly. "All right, Bill Mason, remember we have an agreement, but it's okay to cancel if you want. I promise not to be pushy, but it will make me so *very* happy if you agree to pray with me."

"No, no, I'm ready."

Her voice became low and steady. "Bill, do you believe there really is a God?"

"Sure I do, but I don't think about it much."

"God thinks about you, Bill, every day. But tell me, if you were to die right now, do you think you would go to heaven?"

"Oh, if there's a heaven, I'd probably squeak by. I'm not perfect but I haven't been really bad either." He grinned. "No murder-ones on *my* record."

"The Bible is Gods word, Bill. It tells us that we have *all* sinned and fallen short of God's glory. So there's no getting into heaven on good works."

"Bummer."

Esther bestowed a broad smile. At that moment Bill thought he had never before beheld anything so beautiful as the face that glowed before his eyes. "But the *good* news is it also says that whosoever believes in the Lord Jesus shall have everlasting life. That is called salvation, my dear, and it's a gift."

"That sounds too easy. If I did believe, and I'm not saying I do, how could I let God, er Jesus, know I believe in Him?"

"If your heart opens up to Him, He will know, Bill. We'll begin by saying a prayer together. Put your hand through that little slot under the glass."

There wasn't much room, but he wiggled most of his fingers through the opening. She reached out with both hands and slender warm fingers held him fast. Her large eyes slowly closed and she began, "Dearest Lord, please bless Bill and do a quick work in his heart. If he has not yet received Jesus Christ as his Lord and Savior I pray he will do so now."

Bill shook his head. "But I…"

Esther's blue-gray eyes opened so wide it reminded him of a Keane painting, her gaze tickling gently deep into his soul. "It's all right, Bill." She gave him a gentle squeeze. "If you would like to receive this gift, please repeat after me and take these words into your heart."

Bill felt a calmness come over him. He repeated the prayer, his eyes not straying from her steady gaze. "Dear Jesus, come into my heart and forgive my sins.—Cleanse me and set me free." She nodded. "I thank you for dying for me.—I believe You have risen from the dead and I will see You when you come back. Fill me with the Holy Spirit and change me as You will.—Give me a boldness to preach Your message to the lost.—I am born again and saved for heaven now that I have Jesus in my heart."

Bill fell silent, still transfixed in her gaze. He gave her fingers a little tug. She squeezed back. "Bill, as Christ's minister I am so happy to tell you that your sins have been forgiven. Whenever you find trouble, remember to always run *toward* God, not away, because He loves you so *very* much and has a wonderful plan for your life."

Bill felt a tingling through his body. "A wonderful plan?"

She nodded.

He grinned. "Think His plans for me include you?"

Esther giggled and released his hand with a little slap. "Follow the Spirit. I know it will be a joyful path and I can't wait to see where He will lead you."

The time warning buzzer sounded. "Esther, do you want me to go to church?"

"I think you will find that need in your heart particularly if you first pray in private. One word of advice though. Select a congregation that accepts Jesus as God, fully divine, and no waffling. Also, I think you'll do best with a mentor who is a man, so your church should be run by one." She rose slowly. "God bless you, Bill."

"Remember our deal. Next time it's about you."

She sighed. "I'll keep my word, but you won't like it. See you next week."

IZZY

"What is it now, Izzy? Can't you see I'm busy? I got New York on the line here."

Izzy took his one step into the room. "She's meeting *regular* with him, one on one. They're exchanging papers. I can't sleep, Boss."

Conklin held his hand up to him and spoke into the phone. "Look I said you *should* get them yesterday. No promises. Look, if you don't get your shipment today, take ten percent off. Hold on." He turned to Izzy with a grimace and threw his hand into a "what?" gesture.

"Mr. C, I have someone in place to take care of her. Just need your okay."

"So my Captain can't sleep." He chuckled. "This'll be clean?"

"Oh yeah. Inside the pen and clean. Remember, I'd be the big loser. Nothing could touch you no how."

C went back to the phone. “Yeah, well it *was* going to be that place until you just now said it on the phone. So it’s gonna be different, understand? My man will come by today and fill you in personal. Pleasure doing business with ya.”

Izzy was waiting with his gaze fixed and jaw drooping. C brushed him away with his hand. “Yeah, sure Izzy, be happy. Make it happen. Now get out of here.”

Izzy blew him a kiss and closed the door.

WORKING

Bill leaned on the cubicle wall, looked in on his co-worker, and knocked. “Liz, you look really upset. Anything I can do?”

It’s my boy, Adam in third grade. The school called. He was in a fight and they’re sending him home.”

“Is he all right?”

Liz dabbed at one eye. “Yes, they said, a cut lip but okay. He’s got a key and they’ll wait to make sure he’s inside before the driver leaves.”

“So it’s okay then? You’re just angry?”

“Bill, he’s *seven,* and he’s alone and hurt. I won’t get home for three hours.”

“O shoot, you’re right. I get it. Get out of here, Liz. I see you’re just updating inventory. I can do that for you.”

“I can’t ask you to do that.”

“You didn’t ask. Now shoo.”

Myrna's door clunked shut. She walked down the quiet corridor suddenly aware that her shoes creaked. She looked into a cubicle room with a light still on and walked in. Bill was tapping on his keyboard. "Hey Bill, it's almost six. Is our company in trouble or are you spending your inheritance on the internet?"

He glanced up with a grin. "Almost through, Myrna. Something you want to talk about?"

She rolled a reclining desk chair over to his cubicle entrance and settled in. "I can wait. It's my husband's turn to start fixing dinner."

Bill hit the last key with a "bam". "There, done. "What can I do you for, Ma'am?"

Myrna rocked a little in her chair, and tilted her head to one side. "That was really nice what you did for Liz today."

He sighed. "Is there *anything* happening in this company you don't know about, Myrna?"

"Probably not. For instance I notice you're a changed man too. A few weeks ago you were just happy teaching, but now you've resigned. You're full of energy these days and, the most striking thing is you're relating to new people and making eye contact."

"So," he gestured with his hands. "I'm finally learning to adjust, huh?"

She shook her head. "Nah, no one fools Myrna, Bill. You still visiting that inmate?"

Bill couldn't conceal a smile but lowered his head in an attempt.

"Ha! I thought so. It's none of my business, I know, but I am responsible for sending you there. You were upset about her fighting, right?"

He sighed again. "In confidence, right?"

Her fingers made a twist over her lips. "Sealed, I promise. She's Mrs. Green?"

"Miss Green."

Myrna's eyebrows popped up but she said nothing.

"Esther is just the most fascinating person I've *ever* met. She's truly wonderful. There's a gang in Yard-B run by a woman named Rita. She hates Esther and has her beaten, but this little woman has been learning karate moves to avoid the blows."

"Yeah, gangs always look for domination. Not uncommon. I assume Esther is part of a rival gang?"

Bill laughed and shook his head. "No, no, Rita hates her because she's preaching the gospel and converting inmates to following the Lord. Worse yet, some of these people used to be in Rita's gang."

"Whoa. I work mostly in Yard-A, but I think I've heard of this woman. They call her the 'Evangel of Yard-B'." She shook her head. "Never met her, but I'd love to. In Kairos we do the same thing, but of course we don't sit with them in their cells all day."

Bill squinched his face. "I'd say you could see her on visiting hours, but those are mostly taken up by me."

Myrna settled back in her chair and studied Bill's face. She spoke in a soft velvet tone. "You're in love with her."

"No, no I…"

Bill, I understand, but I have to tell you, it's better to avoid a relationship with an inmate—*any* inmate, even a good Christian. They're often man crazy and will lead you on, and where could it go? Unless she's getting released next month, my advice is to break it off. Seriously, I mean it."

Bill examined the ceiling tiles for a moment. He whispered, "She led me to Christ, Myrna." He bit his quivering lip, closed his eyes and dropped his head.

Myrna shook her head. She got up with a grin and pulled his head against her. "Okay, Bill, I give up. Now I love her too."

HISTORY

Esther bounced through the door, hurried to her seat to greet Bill and placed her hand on the glass. He put his against hers with mutual grins. "How ya doin' Bill?"

"The weeks are getting longer, I think."

She giggled. "Yeah, thanks for going through the prayer with me last week. I *so* hope it brought you and the Lord together. Taking you to Him was especially important to me even though I want everyone to share in the joy He gives. I hope you didn't think I was too aggressive."

"No, Esther, that was profound. I actually felt a change inside me, something peaceful and good. It's hard to explain, but thank you. Haven't heard of a new plan for my life yet, though."

Her eyes brightened. "Oh Bill, I'm so glad to hear that, but you won't get the new plan unless you learn to listen. Ask Him in prayer, but remember, He whispers."

"Anyway, I just wanted to say thank you. You really did something that changed me for the better."

"I didn't do anything myself except invite you and His spirit to come together. It's kinda like I know where this river of Grace is, and I take you for a walk along side of it, and surprise! I just swing my hips and bounce you in."

He chuckled. "That's a nice image." He grinned. "I'll go swimming with you anytime, Esther, but remember today is the day you're going to tell me all about yourself, right?"

Esther rested her head on one hand. "Oh gosh, I know I promised, but now I'm getting really nervous about telling you. This will just be between us, huh?"

"That wasn't part of the deal, my dear."

"But, I'm going to tell you things I've never told *anyone* so promise me you won't start blabbing this to your buddies at the bar."

Bill leaned in and lowered his voice. "Esther, you have earned my *deepest* respect. I would never do anything that might harm or demean you."

She returned a demure smile. "Thank you, Bill. All right, but I'll start with the express version. An ER nurse in

Vegas pulled me in screaming at the front door when I was about a week old. She named me "Green" because I was wrapped in a green blanket, and Ester because the stars were so bright that night. They treated me for crack in my system, and the State farmed me out to an orphanage and then to foster homes. I went through four of them through high school."

"You were that much trouble, huh?"

Esther laughed. "Well, maybe that was part of it, but you get moved around for lots of reasons. They took me out of the third one when they found out I was being molested."

"Oh rats! How old were you?"

"Twelve, but at least the last couple I had was the best of the lot. Strict and demanding but they taught me respect. In high school I found my own life with girlfriends and books. I did a lot of babysitting because I love children and drawing pictures for them. Guess I always wanted some of my own."

"But no high school sweethearts?"

"Nah, I had some chances, but I was afraid of men in those days."

Bill nodded. "No surprise."

"Well, in my senior year I turned eighteen and my stepdad took me to his work place. He taught me how to mix drinks and stuff but I never drank much myself. Whiskey's just awful, isn't it? Anyway, he managed a bar and wanted me to start a life on my own."

"That's good. He was thinking about what would be best for you when you left."

"I thought so, but in retrospect, he was doing what he thought would be best for his *boss*, the guy who owned the bar. Jimmy-the-Boss rarely came by the bar. He owned lots of them, but he told my stepfather he wanted to start dating me."

"Let me guess. He abused you too."

"No, surprisingly he was a real gentleman. I was nineteen and he was late forty something. Jimmy was a big contractor, and built things like schools and churches, you know, commercial buildings. He took me to the best restaurants, operas and charity balls, and bought me expensive presents. At first the only time he would touch me was for a good night kiss on the cheek."

"Weird. I don't get it."

Esther shook her head. "Well, neither did teenage me. I had plenty of book learning, but otherwise I was clueless. I was so flattered that this rich man wanted to be with me, so when he proposed, I wanted a family and just said yes. I mean, where was my life going anyway?"

"Not even a little suspicious? So what was life like with the dirty old man?"

"You said it: weird. We had a quick Justice of the Peace marriage. He put me up in a suburban house with a cook and a maid. I had a car and shopping money. He only came by once a week or so and sometimes he spent the night, so we did have sex once in awhile, but he obviously had plenty of women elsewhere."

"And the point of all that? Did you enjoy life?"

"Really boring. Turned out my job was just to be obedient. I was what they call a trophy wife. He wanted me on his arm when we entertained investors in commercial buildings and charity functions. Jimmy kept his real life a secret so I couldn't answer any questions, but I came to realize what was really going on from what I overheard."

"And that was?"

"That Jimmy was a mobster and ran a huge operation involving drugs and human trafficking. Our marriage was just part of his cover. He really thought I would be happy to just stay home and take my birth control pills."

"Oh, man. So you rebelled, huh?"

"I stopped taking the pills. I knew he didn't want a child, but I did, and I thought he wouldn't really be too upset."

Bill's head snapped up. "Mobsters don't like to be crossed."

Esther studied the floor for a few moments shaking her head. "That's when his true self came out. He showed up at the house with three men when I was three months pregnant and started shouting and slapping me around. Can't repeat what they said. After that the men forced me down on the floor, held me still and gave me a shot."

She put her head in both hands and began to sob. Bill put his fingers under the glass but couldn't touch her. She cried out. "Oh, my baby, my *baby*."

A silent minute passed before Esther wiped her eyes with her sleeve. "Sorry, Bill. I thought I'd put that behind me."

"But what, a shot? They tranquilized you and threw you out? What?"

Esther snuffed and swallowed. Her voice became hoarse. "Later that day I woke up in the hospital. My baby had been ripped out of me."

"Bill stood up, aghast. "They *killed* your child? But that was his son or daughter too. What did the doctor say?

"He said I signed for it, that another doctor said I was suicidal and I had given myself a shot to cause an abortion."

"Couldn't you just walk out on this monster?"

She shook her head. "Take off on Jimmy? No one tries that and lives. I did start walking though, but just to explore my neighborhood. I made friends with Lucia. She's an eighty-two year old widow, I guess eighty-five by now. She listened to all my self-pity, gave me hugs, understanding, and a new backbone. Lucia loved me like a mother, and I learned about Jesus from her. She helped me turn my life around, and I did."

"Let me guess. She gave you the gift you gave me."

"Sure did. I came to a certain knowledge that God is real, that He loves me, and forgives my sins. The Lord's been slowly changing me from the inside just like you, but we're always works in progress." There was a hint of a chuckle. "I guess you can tell."

"No, Esther, that's beautiful, and I think you are wonderful just the way you are right now. But wait, what about the murder-one?"

"I'll get there, but first I want to tell you about Ginny, the maid that was assigned to the house. We became great friends. She's a Christian, and we spent hours together walking and talking. I snuck her out for fun lunches all over town and we tried to learn tennis playing in a public park." She grinned. "We were both awful at it, of course."

"You snuck her out?"

"Yup. I cleaned up the upstairs for her in the morning so we could have our afternoons together. The car had a tracker but I was allowed to take it to the mall, remember?"

"Sure, go on."

"I could also walk places from the mall lot. Once I walked back to the hospital three blocks away and got a look at my record." Esther looked up, blew out through her cheeks and went on. "My baby was a boy. He was a boy. I named him David after that near perfect man in the Bible."

"Aw shucks, Esther." He reached through the under glass space. This time he found her fingers.

"After the abortion, Jimmy was getting really cold to me. He stopped taking me anywhere, but he insisted I learn how to shoot a pistol. He claimed it was necessary since I was alone in the house at night, and sent his man Isadore to take me to the range twice a week."

"Hey, time's almost up. What about the murder thing? You accidentally shoot someone with it?"

"No, no. One night Isadore showed up with two other men. They had 'shark eyes' like the ones who attacked me when I was pregnant. I panicked of course. I had no idea what was happening. I almost got away out the door, but they got me, and held me down, injected me with something. Last thing I remember Izzy said was 'Shoot her dog if you can find it'."

The two minute buzzer sounded and Bill pounded the shelf in front of him. "Oh God, that's terrible—*terrible!* What did they do to you this time?"

"This time I woke up all groggy in my car in some other town. Police had smashed the window in and were dragging me out. There were lots of drugs around and that pistol was in my purse next to me. I started to thank them but they handcuffed me and took me to the station. Long story short: Jimmy's gang had shot someone with my gun and made it look like I did it."

Bill shot up, hands on the glass, "Okay, that's it. I'm getting you *out* of there."

Ester stood up in front of him, terror on her face. She leaned in, shaking her head. "Oh, *no* Bill, no. It's just for you to know. *Please* don't even think of trying to do anything on the outside. They'll *kill* you if you try and God wants me here for His own purpose. I'm sure of it."

"Crazy talk, Esther. You deserve to be free. Just wait."

She began to pound on the glass and two guards came from behind to pull her away. "No, no Bill." She shouted. "They really *will* kill you, and then it would be all my fault. I love you. You can't die. I couldn't stand that. Please, don't."

The guards pulled her away from the window. She shouted, "Promise me you won't do anything. I'll tell you more next week."

Bill sat in the dark parking lot, his thoughts confused, his heart racing. *They used her, framed her. Rotten scum!*

He slammed the steering wheel. *Bastards! Here she is, the most beautiful person, like ever, and they treated her like garbage. Sure they're dangerous. Well duh—they're mobsters.*

He slumped back and sighed. *What could one man do against the likes of them? And she's right. I'll probably get myself killed if I'm not careful. One more dead warrior fighting for a just cause.*

Bill sat quietly for awhile. He tilted his head skyward. *Any man with common sense would drive away right now and never talk to her again. But she said something else important and lowered her voice when she said it—hit me in my gut.* He grinned. *A woman this, this wonderful woman—did she really mean she loves me?* He studied the visitors streaming out of the exit. *Nah, probably "loves", more like: "I love my teacher or I love to draw."*

Still, when she said it, those big, beautiful, pleading eyes of hers were looking right at me. He grinned again.

THE SHIV

The line in the corridor was moving slower than usual toward the exercise yard. The guards may have been looking for something and took their time checking the attendance list at the door. Esther knew that slow moving lines meant danger, so she was on her guard. Should one of Rita's women maneuver closer, she would slide back around someone else.

A new inmate had stepped out of line and was coughing. The line was passing her by, but she stepped back in as Esther came by.

There! A flash, and an arm sliced toward her. Knife! Esther jumped, spinning back and to one side and crashing between the two women behind her. One of them cuffed her cheek. "Hey, *watch it,* Greenie."

The new woman didn't turn around but kept walking in front of her. "Sorry," she said to the people she bumped, and delicately moved back another row.

Esther's left arm was stinging and she looked down to see a bleeding slash. She held pressure on it with the edge of her shirt and kept moving with the crowd, but she kept an eye on the would-be killer ahead of her.

This woman was nonchalantly chatting with women next to her as if nothing had happened. The ID checker at the door just smiled at her and waved her into the yard.

Most of the inmates were walking or jogging around the perimeter, but some were just standing around. Esther saw Rita in the far corner with some of her inner circle and walked straight for her.

"Rita, got a moment?"

She chuckled. "Well Weenie-Greenie, you've got guts. I'll give you that. Thought you'd just stroll over for a chat, huh?"

"Did you put out an order to kill me, Rita?"

"What?" She bent her head down to study the delicate but defiant creature pouting up at her. "You gotta know that's not my style, little one. I'm having too much fun with you to spoil a good thing."

Esther bared her bleeding forearm. "Well, someone just did. That knife was aimed at my heart."

"Who?"

She gestured with her head. “That one jogging over there. She’s the one with the black hair in a bun.”

“New transfer from upstate. Names Nina Olivetti. Haven’t had our welcome chat yet.” Rita squinted. “This is interesting. So, someone wants you dead. You’re probably a witness against someone, huh?”

Esther nodded. “You could say that.”

Rita grinned. “Well you’ve just made my dull day more fun, but no one hurts anyone in this yard without my say so.”

“Ah, that’s so reassuring.”

Rita tried to conceal a smile. “Tell you what, Greenie, I’m declaring a temporary truce. My people will switch to protective duty until I find out what’s going on. That means…” She chuckled. “You can quit the ballet practice when they get close to you.”

“I’ll trust you, Rita.”

That produced a puzzled expression. “And if Olivetti has a shiv, I’ll turn her in. Maybe the guards will even give me a Brownie Point. Course you’ll owe me too, sister.”

“Most grateful for your help, Rita.”

“Tell me something, Greenie. Why don’t you just give up this preaching to people? You’ll never get a gang as big as mine and you’ll stay a lot healthier.”

"Because saving their lives in this world and the next serves the Lord and makes my life worthwhile."

"Yeah, well lookie here. I'm the one saving *your* life right now."

Esther grinned. She started to walk away but turned and spoke over her shoulder. "We should talk more. I could return the favor."

"Hey, don't think when this is over we're not going back to our old time fun."

PLAN B FROM MR C

Conklin sat squeezed into a corner booth in his very own smoke-filled lounge. Two adoring pole dancers squirmed around on either side of him. He looked up at Izzy who appeared out of the gloom and stood before him. "Now what? Can't you see I'm *busy.*"

"I can, but it's important, boss. And these two cuties have to change. They're due on stage in ten minutes."

"Ahh (expletive!)" He lightly bit one on the shoulder. "Okay you two, scram. Just come right back when you're gig's over." He reached for his cigar and gave it a puff. "This better be good, Iz."

"Plan A didn't work."

"Really. I thought your inside girl was good."

"Oh Nina's the best. Never failed before, but this girl slipped away. She's got help of her own on the inside. Nina got caught with her shiv and they sent her back where she came from."

Mr. C emitted a blue smoke cloud. His gaze followed it to the ceiling. He scowled. "You figure our target's in with the LA mob now, right?"

Izzy nodded.

"Izzy, I know you'll be the first to burn here, but if you go down you could take a pile of us with you. How's she really gonna make trouble?"

"I'm pretty sure she blabbed to the teacher when he visited. They were shouting at each other last time."

"Yeah, but an outside hit could expose us. Track this guy first. Make sure he's really trouble before you go to plan B, okay?"

"Already sent two guys to work him, but I'd sleep better if he just disappeared."

Conklin blew out a breath and made his lips blubber. "Yeah, yeah. I know how you think, Izzy. Your problem is you always think with your trigger finger instead of your head."

ANXIETY

Bill sat in the visitor's lounge trying to read one of the old magazines. *This was the longest week ever. Don't really know whether she'll be happy or furious when I tell her.*

The next six they called didn't include him, and he complained to the receptionist and pointed to a visitor. "That woman was behind me when I came in."

"Sorry mister, we got two registrars and her's finished first. You'll be next." He swished his head in frustration and went back to his seat. *That'll make it forty five minutes and who knows: she might not even see me now.*

Finally the next round was called. Bill waited another two anxious minutes before Esther appeared frowning in the doorway. Her nose still listed to one side, but at least she had no new bruises. She slid into her chair and glared at him for a moment. "You've been up to something, haven't you?"

He shrugged. "Well yes, but I think you'll be pleased."

"Bill, they sent someone inside here to *kill* me three days ago. It's probably just because I'm talking to you." She bared the gash on her forearm. "Just missed."

He half stood up, hand on his mouth. "Oh my God, Esther. I'm so sorry. I know this group is ruthless. Can't the guards give you extra protection?"

She motioned for him to sit, her expression becoming softer. "It's okay now. They won't try again in here. I'm more worried about you doing something stupid out *there*."

"Stupid as in trying to rescue you?"

"Exactly. This Vegas mob is very big and powerful. Walking into some lawyer's office and trying to get my case opened will put your name on a tombstone for sure. Besides, if my former husband was the guilty one, he died in a narc shootout last year and won't be testifying."

"I know. The headlines read 'Philanthroper dies in crossfire.' There were only hints of mob connections."

Esther sighed and leaned back in her seat. "You seem to be well informed, Bill. So just what *have* you been up to?"

"No lawyers, Esther—at least not yet. I was referred to a high priced private investigator, one who's not afraid of gangsters. We met only twice, each time in a different public place. He calls himself Jake."

She leaned in and lowered her voice. "And what did this Jake tell you?"

"So far he's just seen the trial record. He already knew about Jimmy and Isadore. Told me there's no question you're innocent, but proving it is another thing. The trial was a sham. Your public defender avoided any questions of substance."

"Look, Bill—please just leave this alone. Of course I'd love to be free, but believe it or not, I'm at peace with being in here. Please don't go to any lawyers."

"I *know* you are, Esther." He paused and bit his lip. "But that's because of the hugely wonderful person you are."

They sat, locked in each other's gaze. "Bill, I'm not so wonderful. I just…" A tear began to work its way down one cheek. "*You're* the one who's wonderful. No man has ever tried to help me. I don't understand."

"Understand this. I will never stop being your friend and I will move heaven and earth to give you the life you deserve. Why are you crying?"

"B-because I've never felt like this before. I guess you've already spent like a *lot* of money on Jake, and you know the danger. You'd even risk your life to save me?"

Bill wiggled his hand through the slot so they could grasp fingers. "Oh yes."

JAKE

As instructed, Bill sat on an assigned park bench near his work place munching on a bag lunch and reading a newspaper. This bench was back to back with another one. A man in a loud Hawaiian shirt sat behind him smoking a pipe. Bill wasn't even sure it was Jake until he spoke.

"Well, Bill, I've looked into this deeper. I do this for a living, but you should consider dropping the idea of taking these people on. I see you've hired a man from Black Eagle security to follow you around, but you'll be going up against a large criminal organization. No one can guarantee your safety. No one. And now that I see we're dealing with the mob, my fee from now on will be fifty percent more. You still in?"

"All the way, Jake."

He heard a chuckle from behind. "Good man, Bill."

"So, anything new to tell me?"

"Okay first, if your security people haven't told you already, you have one or two tags from the Vegas syndicate following you at all times. That guy leaning on the phone pole with a cigarette is one of them. Keep eating your lunch and don't look back."

Bill spoke with his mouth full. "Think he'll just shoot me?"

Jake released a deep laugh. "Nah, you're not a threat yet, but you will be."

"Oh goodie."

"Our plan should be to get the old trial set aside on the basis of new evidence. Green's public defender was either incompetent or more likely in collusion. The examining officer found no blood spatters in the deceased's apartment despite a shot through the head. Autopsy showed evidence that his hands and feet had been bound. Clearly he was executed professionally and moved back to his residence."

"Clearly?"

"I think so. Also I checked Esther's admitting exam in prison. Her so called 'tracks' from heroine addiction were all recent punctures, and even more significantly, Ms. Green never had any withdrawal symptoms."

"But would that be enough to get a new trial?"

"I'm not a lawyer, but I think it could throw out the whole case, maybe a mistrial. What is particularly important is the fact that her defense lawyer never followed up on *any* of these facts."

"But it was her gun, right?"

"More like a gun she had used in the past. The surveillance camera at a nearby range shows two men trying to teach her to shoot on three occasions. She was clumsy and it took her two hands to even hold the gun up."

"Maybe one of the men was the actual shooter."

"Who knows, but one of the men is Isadore Croft, at least a captain in the Vegas mob, maybe higher. Oh, and get this: there were two large partial prints on the barrel tip. Most likely they weren't hers and her lawyer never even asked if they were checked."

"Wow, Jake, that all fits perfectly with what Esther told me."

"Truth is truth."

Bill looked up at the treetops and exhaled through puffed out cheeks. "Okay then, what's the next step to get her out?"

"I'm going to drop a crumpled piece of paper near you when I get up. It's the lawyer I'd recommend, assuming cost is no object. Use your office line to make the appointment."

"Won't I be followed when I go there?"

"He's in a high rise building in San Diego, but there's a Zabar's restaurant in a smaller building next door. Go in that way and up the stairs. The two buildings connect on the second floor."

"Do you think my phone is tapped?"

"Assume that it is. That's why I said to use a back line at your work. Unless they think you're getting the case reopened, they probably won't go after you."

"Sounds like your work is done."

"Not quite, Bill. I need to look into possible surveillance cameras near the deceased's apartment, but it's likely they've been erased since it's three years later. With your permission, I will also investigate anything your lawyer requests."

"Great work, Jake. I can see Esther dancing into my arms already."

LEGAL EAGLE

Zabar's was already busy before eleven with lunch preparations. A few earlier customers sat by the windows with their coffee and Danish while the waiters clattered plates and set up tables.

Bill went to the service bar and got a coffee to go. He tarried awhile by the back stairs observing all who came and went. When he was satisfied no one had followed him in he went up and crossed over to the office building.

Bill exited his elevator at the seventeenth floor with a woman in a business suit and a heavy briefcase. She strode through the massive mahogany doors. He checked the discrete brass plaque beside them. *Yup, Anderson and Haggith.*

The spacious reception area could have graced the pages of Architectural Digest with its potted plants and understated victorianesque elegance. He approached the receptionist who sported a cheerful, expectant grin. She looked down and pressed her com button. "Uh, William Mason to see you, Mister Anderson."

Big smile for Bill. "Oh, yes sir, he will call for you in a moment. I see you have coffee. There's more in that corner and fresh pastries." With a toss of her hair she said, "You should try the crumb cake. It's my *favorite*."

Bill chose to just sit on a divan against the wall. *One visit here and I'll lose a month's salary. Sure hope Jake is right about him.*

After a few minutes, an impeccable gray pin-stripe suit marched into his peripheral vision. His rugged face and salt and pepper hair reminded him more of a sailor than a lawyer. His broad smile and twinkling eyes made Bill think he was about to be invited to play tennis. "You must be Bill Mason. I am Pierce Anderson."

Bill stood up to shake his hand. "Uh, yes Sir, eleven o' clock appointment."

The lawyer chuckled. "Of course. Call me Pierce." He gestured Bill to follow him. "Park that cold coffee. There's fresh Sumatra Dark inside."

They walked past his office into a spacious conference room with glass walls. Bill poured half a cup from the side bar, peered down at the street for a moment and sat. A few folders lay on the table and Mr. Anderson spread out some pages from one of them. "Bill, I have to say, the information Jake sent me is most interesting."

"Oh, before we get started, uh, Pierce, I must tell you that my funds are limited. All I have is a hundred twenty thousand, but I did bring the two thousand retainer you asked for."

Pierce made a gentle eye contact. "You're a good man, Bill. Look, there's much more work to be done but I'm confident from what I've seen that I can get your, uh, friend released as a mistrial especially when we get to analyze the evidence bag. The retainer is for our consultation and my preliminary research. I will not ask you for more. If Ms. Green agrees to take me on as her counsel, I will handle her case pro bono."

Bill jerked back. "What! I just said I would pay you. Why would you take the case for free?"

"Ms. Green has no assets. It's the right thing to do. Beyond that, and only if she wishes, I will bring a wrongful imprisonment suit at thirty per cent contingency."

Bill grinned. "Wow."

"Let me begin by giving you a little background on myself. Twenty years ago I was a prosecutor and had some success at putting several members of organized crime behind bars. Over the past ten years I have been with this firm as a defense attorney. You probably know we have had some very high profile clients. I have become familiar with these, let's say, high end criminals from both sides."

"And I will be so grateful if you can get Esther out of there."

"I'm optimistic, but I make no promises. First, I must counsel you that you face considerable personal danger from the Syndicate. However, once Ms. Green has *won* her case they will not touch her or you since it would expose them further. Before that both of you will be seen as prey in need of disposal."

"Prey?"

"Let me put it another way. Rather than just rely on the best counsel money can buy, they make a point to silence potential witnesses."

Bill looked up at the ceiling. "Wish everyone would stop telling me that. I did hire Black Eagle Security, and anyway, Esther also led me to expect eternal life."

Pierce was quietly grinning. Bill added: "You're a Christian, aren't you?"

"Yes, but I'm surprised how few of my clients ask. Shall we move on to our next step?"

"Oh sure. I'm feeling much better now, except of course, about that 'getting shot down in the street thing.'"

"Okay, I'm going to give you some papers for Ms. Green to sign. Normally a client would come to me first, but in this case it will be better to give you power of attorney. If she does hire me as counsel, I will visit her in prison of course."

"Then what?"

"Then I can file a mistrial and a release petition. It will give me access to depositions and the all important physical evidence."

"Oh God I sure hope this works."

Pierce handed Bill a Manila envelope. "There are three copies for her to sign. They also authorize you to act as her agent. I suggest you keep her copy as well as yours rather than letting her take it back into prison. Mail the other one back to me." He stood up to shake hands.

Bill was bright-eyed. "Thank you *so* much, Mr. Anderson."

"Pierce, Bill. We'll be in touch soon."

Bill retraced his steps back out of the buildings clutching the folder. Sitting at a table by the door in Zabar's, he recognized the now familiar face of a mobster spy.

DÉTENTE

Two muscular women dragged Esther, struggling and protesting, across the exercise yard. She was still trying to lunge free when they came to a halt in front of Big Rita. They let her go with a push but stood ready to grab her again.

Esther shook herself like a wet puppy and jerked the wrinkles out of her tan pullover. "That's *right!* Unhand me, you ruffians."

Rita was laughing. "You do know, you're the most amusing person in the yard."

Esther raised up her fists 1920 boxing style and did a little dance. "Yeah? Put up your dukes. Come on, come on."

Ruth put her hand over her eyes. "Oh stop. I'll die laughing. Look I just want to talk."

Esther listed her head to one side. "Oh." She produced a wide eyed grin.

Rita pointed her finger. "Ngami, that is Nancy, told me what's really going on here. She used to be with me as you know. I had assumed you were gathering recruits to take over this yard. You were from the Vegas mob after all, but now I get it. You're just a religious freak and Vegas wants you dead, right?"

"Uh huh, and Jesus freak? Guilty as charged."

"Yeah, I don't care about that, but enemy of my enemy? I'm with you now. You know that writer's group? There were two Vegas gals and one of ours in there. They're all *buddies* with each other now. Didn't think that was even possible. You've got something going on in our little tank, don't you, Miss cutie?"

Esther looked up at the big woman. "Oh, Rita, you're right, but one day I'll tell you all about my secret weapon."

"Yeah? Your tricks at getting followers sounds interesting. We'll talk about that some other time, but for now, the war's over." She put a huge smelly arm around her shoulders, turned and announced to the unbelieving onlookers. "Listen up. From now on I want you all to know that Esther Greenie--er, Green and all her friends are my friends too."

Not to miss the opportunity, Esther quickly raised an arm over her head. "Praise the Lord!"

HOPE

Esther slid the papers under the glass. "I wasn't going to sign these, Bill, but things have changed in here. I shouldn't think I'm indispensable. There are five others I've trained to do the Lord's work in Yard B, and now Big Rita is positively chummy."

"So no one's going to get beaten up?"

"No, isn't it great?" She lowered her eyebrows. "But know this: if they find out you're working to help me, or if you're threatened in any way, the deal is *off.* I'll stay in here."

Bill pouted and slid the papers part way back. "Well, if you have no *other* reason to get out, perhaps you should stay in the clink then."

Esther laughed. "Oh, Bill, you know I want to get out and be with you, more than anything, but I just need to know you're going to be safe. Also, I'm not sure about God's will for me."

"Don't you consider that Rita suddenly turning pleasant is a miracle as great as parting the Red Sea?"

They gazed into each other's eyes until their expressions softened. Esther wiggled her fingers under the glass so he could hold them. "So, Bill, I see this paper gives you power of attorney. Does that mean I'm in your charge?"

Bill waved the papers with his free hand. "Yup, got to do *everything* I say."

Esther returned a twinkly-eyed chuckle. He slipped the documents into his briefcase. "Really, all it's for is so I can relay information between you and your attorney."

She withdrew her hand and rested her chin on it. "Tell me the truth, Bill; do you really think there's even a slight chance Pierce can get me released?"

"Oh I think so, my dear. He seems quite confident. I am too, and I will never, *ever* lie to you."

"Nor I to you, Bill. But doesn't my attorney have to prove someone else murdered that man? I don't want you to risk opening a *new* case cause then they'd go after you for sure."

"Oh, no. Here's the thing. If he just proved you had an incompetent lawyer, he could get a new jury trial, *but* if he produces evidence showing there's *no way* you could be guilty, the judge could request the District Attorney to dismiss the charges. Your second trial would be a quick one right in his chambers."

Esther nodded. “That’s exciting. Maybe the Lord *does* want me to start carrying His good news outside these walls.”

“Ah yes, my sweet freckle-nosed girlfriend. I’ve been praying He does.”

REALITY

Bill picked up the phone and called his Black Eagle guard who sat in the car parked ahead of him. "Any sign we've been followed?"

"None Sir, but remain cautious. I'll keep an eye on your car."

"Look, I'm running late. I'm going to take a quick jog straight across into the main building."

Come on elevator. Man, I'm so excited. Pierce has had the papers for almost a week. I'd sure like to give Esther some good news tomorrow.

The receptionist stood up and came around her counter to greet him. No smile this time. "Good morning Mr. Mason, Mr. Anderson will see you in his office this time. Follow me."

She knocked on a door in the hallway, opened it and gestured him inside. Pierce rose, shook hands and indicated a seat next to his large oak desk. He was stone-faced. "Bill, we've had a setback."

He could feel the pulses in his temples. "But wh—what? You were so confident."

Pierce nodded. I know, and I'm sorry I projected enthusiasm so early. It's the old prosecutor in me. I see evil and I'm always confident I can crush it."

"But what's changed?"

"What *hasn't* changed is organized crime. They are well financed, paranoid, and have long arms in many places. Still, I didn't anticipate this one. The evidence bag for Ms. Green's case is missing from the police Evidence Room."

"What, no record of it?"

"There's an inventory and a number registration, but the bag itself is not where it's supposed to be. They searched the room carefully. No luck."

"And we have to have it?"

"Really, yes. It's the sum of provable details that would win our case. Without them, we have a dead drug dealer shot with Esther's gun, found in her possession when she was high on morphine."

"But that was just a *setup*." Bill felt an anxious pressure to go to the window. He got up, leaned against the glass and stared at the street below. "Pierce, level with me. Are you telling me it's hopeless?"

"No, of course there's still some hope, but we have work to do. I have asked the police to activate an internal investigation, and I'll have someone do a more thorough search of the Evidence Room. It's difficult to get past the room's security, and that bag had a revolver in it. It's still possible that it's hidden in that room somewhere."

"What's in the bag that's so important?"

"That pouch has things never introduced at trial. There is a sample of under nail scrapings and blood from the knuckles of the deceased. Also there are six autopsy photos. Supposedly they are duplicates, but the original report only has one photo."

Bill was watching his car parked on the street below. Two men with backpacks were standing beside it. "Is there anything I can do?"

"Jake still in your employ?"

"Sure."

"He might be the best choice to do another search of the Evidence Room. Also, have him track down some people from the trial for us. Maybe we can get their depositions. I'll give you a list and inst…"

"Hey! The two guys who were next to my car are running into this building and my guard is chasing them."

"I'll get building security."

Bill took out his cell phone to call his guard, but stopped. A boy on a bicycle pulled up right beside his car. Bill switched to photo and took his picture. The boy took something from the handlebar basket and dropped to the ground behind the car."

"Pierce. Some kid just slid under my car."

He joined Bill at the window. "Maybe he's fixing his bike and we just can't see."

"No way. He just got up and he doesn't have the black thing in his hand anymore. Look, now he's pedaling away." He took another picture.

"Okay, let's not be paranoid, but a bomb is a real possibility. I'll get the police."

WAITING

"Oh Esther, I'm sorry. I know it's been weeks since we hired a lawyer and there's no real breakthrough yet. We did get one deposition and I'll tell you about it in a moment. For now, lets you and I stay hopeful and prayerful."

"I'm sorry too, but maybe it's God's will to keep me here after all."

Bill gave her a scrunchy-face. "Now stop talking that way. Think about the first thing you'll do when you walk out of here. What would that be?"

Esther closed her eyes, took a big breath, and squirmed her fingers under the glass so Bill could hold them. "Free again, huh? I would raise my arms up, dance in circles and praise the Lord." She leveled her gaze at Bill. "But what would *you* do, my dear?"

"You mean *will* do. I love you, Esther, so I will hold you tight against me and never, *ever* let you go."

Their eyes locked and she put her other hand flat against the glass. He placed his against hers, and for a silent moment together. the glass wall disappeared.

Esther slowly withdrew her hand. "Pierce met with me the other day. I wish we could meet in that place. They have a private room for attorneys and clients."

Bill chuckled. "And you *know* why they'd never let the two of us in there."

Esther grinned. Her gaze darted around the room. "But you have power of attorney, don't you?"

"Not with *that* much power, my darling."

She pouted. "Oh fudge. Well, what about that deposition you mentioned?"

Bill ruffled his hair. "Oh yes, and this is hopeful. Pierce's associate got a deposition from the Medical Examiner who did the autopsy. He said it was clear there had been a fight and the man had his hands and feet bound. The deceased had hit someone, too. He had blood on his knuckles, and skin under his fingernails."

"So they can prove he fought with someone?"

"Should have, but the DA told him not to run a DNA test. 'Spare the cost,' he said. 'We'll get a conviction anyway.' Pierce said that was weird behavior for a DA."

"But that test would have proved my innocence."

"Exactly, but the DA did nothing illegal. And now he's a US Representative, by the way, Congressman Peter Smith."

"Really? And I bet no one checked his campaign contributions."

"Well, one good thing. Pierce says the new DA is a real straight shooter."

"Look, Bill, I want to get out of course, but not at any cost. What keeps me awake at night is the possibility that these awful people will see what you're doing and connect it with the possibility of a case against them. You'd tell me if anything suspicious happens, like they're interested in you, right?"

"You mean like the bomb they put under my car last week?"

Esther screamed and stood up, her hand over her mouth. She stood, quivering. "That's it. It's *over!*"

Bill half stood and put his face close to the glass. "Calm down, Dear. We found it in time and no one was hurt."

"No, *no!* You don't get it do you?" She stamped her foot. A guard approached and grabbed her arm. "They will *kill* you, Bill. I won't have it. I want you to stop *everything* right now, and I mean the lawyers, the detective, *everything*. Go away. Don't ever come back here, *ever*."

"Esther, Dear, don't worry. I can take care of myself."

The guard began pulling her back to the exit. "I don't have the strength for this. Forget you ever knew me, Bill. Have a good life. I won't see you again."

The door closed behind Esther, and Bill remained staring ahead, his jaw agape. Another guard took his arm and escorted him away.

DEAR ESTHER

Dear Esther:

I was shocked when you wouldn't meet me today. It's been a week and I thought you would have calmed down by now. I understand why you're worried, but I have all kinds of help to keep me safe. Besides, I thought you understood that your getting released might open up a new case, but they'll keep us in protective custody unlit it's over.

Esther, you know how much you mean to me, and I know you care for me too. Shouldn't we just talk this over? Pierce and I can't proceed with your release unless you give approval.

Darling, I'm just aching to see you. Look, I'll visit you next Saturday and I can answer any questions, okay?

With love,
Bill

WEEK TWO

Esther Darling, this is awful. Why won't you see me? I spoke to Myrna and she thinks you believe you're keeping me alive by dropping your release effort and staying in prison. But I don't want to live without you. I'm not sleeping. They caught me crying in my cubicle today.

The prison people said you were in the infirmary when I came to visit, but I don't know if that's true. I hope you are well. Esther, I'm praying for you every day. You taught me how to do that. Oh God, please let me see you on Saturday.

Love Always,
Bill

LISTEN

Blessed is he who perseveres under trial, because he will receive

The crown of life God promised to those who love Him. Jas 1:12

A man lay curled up in the front of the empty church sobbing. The pastor walked out of a side door toward him, knelt down and gently placed his arm around his shoulders.

Bill sat up suddenly. "I'm sorry—I…" his voice came in spasms. "I must—I must be disturbing you."

"No, no. This fits my routine. I wait in my office for someone to lie down and cry at the altar. When they start pounding the floor and wailing, I come over and ask to help."

"It's (hic) routine?"

"Okay, this is the first time ever, but I do want to help if I can. You're Mr. Mason, right? You sit in the back and keep to yourself."

"No one can help me, Pastor. She left me (hic) and she's right too. She loves me and what she's doing will probably save my life."

Pastor offered a hand up. "Come on to my study. You need a soft chair to talk from."

He walked Bill hand over shoulder to the side room and gestured for him to sit. "I call this my 'crying chair'." He pulled up a stool, handed him a box of tissues, and sat in front of him. "So, you said she loves you, but she left you anyway. What were her last words?"

Bill didn't answer. He sat, head down, shaking it side to side. "Here Bill, have some cool lemon water. It'll help replace the half pint you left out there on the floor."

Bill took a few gulps and handed the glass back. "Her last words were 'pretend you never knew me' and 'don't come back'-- something like that."

"Harsh, but if she loves you, perhaps she doesn't really mean it."

"She means it, Reverend Tim."

"Just Tim, please. I can't promise I can bring her back, but please tell me about this woman."

"She's in prison for murder. Framed. I'm *sure* I can get her out, but when the mob tried to kill me she says she'll stay in there so they'll quit trying to bump me off. Any ideas?"

Bill stared at the wide eyed pastor for a moment. “Didn’t think so.”

Pastor Tim let out a big breath. “Well, Bill, I’m really good at giving advice for the lovelorn and the ‘they fired me without cause’ thing. But your problem seems to be a bit more, uh, complex, but I have the time if you do. Maybe it would help if you could start from the beginning?”

Bill began his story with losing his teaching position in Connecticut and filled in all the details to Tim’s rapt attention. “I just love her more than life, Tim, and I’ve prayed too. Esther’s the one who brought me from just saying, ‘Oh yeah, I’m a Christian’ to really knowing about Christ’s salvation. Every day I pray God will do *something* about what she’s doing now, change her mind or something, but nothing happens.”

“So you don’t think prayer works?”

“Hasn’t.”

“Bill, a situation like yours cannot be solved by any human means. Have you told God that you will accept His will for you and Esther?”

“Accept it? No. I should, huh.”

“Accept His will. And when you do, pray in obedience. Ask Him what is His will for your life too. I do know this: God loves you and wants what's best for you, Bill. Just be quiet and ready to listen to Him."

"Listen?"

"Yes, He speaks in many ways, but pay attention. Most of the time you'll find He whispers."

"Yeah. Esther said that too."

WEEK THREE

Dearest Esther:

I desperately hope you are not throwing my letters away, but perhaps it is best if I never know. The thought that we have this connection at least gives me some comfort even though you still won't see me.

I want to tell you about a breakthrough I had thanks to the good advice of my pastor. In my prayers for our reconciliation I had been asking God to do something. That was wrong. I didn't realize that God would actually take the time to listen and speak. I guess I should have.

I am beginning to understand that I may never see you again, but I told the Lord that I would accept whatever is His will. Last night

He spoke to me in a dream. Wow! Just four words, but He said, "Stand by your love."

I'm still working on what that really means, but I think He is telling me not to give up on us. And, my Darling, you do know that I will never stop loving you, not ever. No matter how long those ugly prison walls remain between us, I will always stand by you.

Esther, you are my forever love, and I will try to see you every week for as long as I am alive unless you write and tell me to stop. But right now I'm really, really hoping for this Saturday.

Love always,
Me

BIG RITA

Esther jogged around the exercise yard Monday morning, her mind swirling between thoughts about freedom, saving Bill from death, and God's will. One of Rita's officers reached out a lanky hand to stop her. "Hey Greenie, Boss wants to talk to you."

Esther bent over hands-on-knees and caught her breath. "Don't I usually get two of you guys to drag me over there? I could use the rest."

"She's in the guard shack. Just go, huh?"

The shack was a small elevated structure sitting on the ground just big enough for two guards to sit and keep a watch on the exercising inmates. Esther paused at its steps and looked up at Rita who was sitting on one of the two chairs. "What can I do for you today, oh Mistress of Pain?"

"Please, come on up and have a seat." Esther's eyes grew wide. This didn't sound like Rita.

She climbed up and sat in the only other chair. "The guards let you sit in here?"

"Sure. They'll do what I want." Rita pointed. "See that one? She's the one assigned for today over there in the corner. They all know I could ask twenty women to jump on them so mostly they behave. Besides, I help them keep the peace."

Esther did not respond. They sat quietly before Rita continued. "You've been looking like a drowned rat lately—crying in corners and such like. You dying of cancer or what?"

"I'm better now. God's helping me cope. You brought me here to ask that?"

"Course not. Look, I just want a private speak witcha. This a good place."

"Sure, Rita. And I should thank you for calling off your persuaders."

Rita squirmed a bit in her chair and coughed. "You're welcome. Won't happen again. Heck, smashing you didn't slow you down noways."

Esther smiled slightly. "Have you felt I'm threatening your control?"

"Yeah, you've gained quite a bunch of followers. Lots of em used to be mine. My lieutenants hated hearing that God message all the time and tried to shut you up. You took plenty of beatings, so why didn't you just give up?"

"Because God's will to save his children is more important than my bruises."

Rita stared out at the inmates for awhile. She spoke without turning her head. "You're the toughest woman I've ever met, little lady and that's saying something. I understand you think you're doing good for people. I have to respect you for that."

"Care to be persuaded by God's message yourself?"

"Another time, maybe. Do you know Pacy McGill?"

"Sure, woman's wrestling team and weight lifter. Almost made the Olympic team but was arrested for assault and using drugs. Nancy told me about her."

"Pacy was one of my top five. Came blubbering to me yesterday sayin' she couldn't work for me no more. Didn't care if I killed her cause she found the Lord."

"Praise God."

"Yeah, well I'm glad *you're* happy. Her cell's next to Ngami Bhutto. She's the one who worked some of your magic on her. Ngami, or Nancy, used to be on my team years ago—suppose you know that too. Now she's your number one, right?"

Esther chuckled. "We don't have a number system, but Nancy's my good friend."

"Well whatever you're doing, you've built one hell of a gang in here, and twelve of them were on my payroll." Rita moved her face close to Esther and lowered her brows and voice. "Look, I'll put two grand in your account if you'll tell me what you *really* used to persuade these people."

Esther covered her mouth to hide the grin. "That's an interesting offer. I'll have to think about it."

The guard had come back and leaned on the door frame. Rita spoke in a fast whisper. "Uh, we gotta go. Three's tops, Greenie. Meet me here in two days. The Wednesday guard will give us all day if we need it."

THE COMMAND

Listen to His voice and hold fast to Him,
For the Lord is your life. Dt 30: 20

Bill stood at the prison registration counter biting his lip. The black woman behind the counter rolled up the whites of her eyes. "Now don't get your hopes up, Mr. Mason, but so far today we haven't got a cancellation. We all pulling for ya..." She turned to the woman next to her. "Right, Stella?" Stella smiled and gave him a thumbs up.

Bill shrugged. "Okay, I'll wait, but sometimes the cancellation comes at the last minute, doesn't it?"

"True, but you jes sit down and relax. Less we hear otherwise, you'll be in the next group."

"No problem, Mary. But just so you know, I *always* have my hopes up."

Ten minutes passed. Mary shook two fists overhead and grinned. "Still can't promise she'll show, but you can go on in now."

Bill sat in the booth and realized how many weeks had past since he made it to the visitor's chair. His heart was beginning to pound. The door on the far side of the glass opened, and there she was: gaunt, red-eyed—absolutely beautiful.

Esther ran to his station, crunched down in the seat and slammed her hand against the glass. She sat, choking and crying, her eyes pleading, unable to speak.

It took a few moments before she rasped out, "Oh God, I've hurt you so very much. I've been *so* foolish, *so* selfish. Please forgive me Bill. Please."

He leaned forward and they did a "glass kiss." "Esther, my darling. There is nothing to forgive. I completely understand how you feel. I really do."

They slid down into their seats, but they each kept one hand on the glass. "Felt. I feel differently now. I realize how selfish I've been."

"Selfish?"

"Yes, I was saving *myself* the pain and guilt of losing you, and I never let myself think I could be getting out of here. I was actually enjoying being a suffering martyr in my mind, and that was selfish too. I tried to control the situation, but it's not my right to force your decisions. Your life is in God's hands, not mine."

"Esther, I realize what you were giving up to save my life. It's just that I'd really rather die than not be with you."

They stopped. It was time to enjoy a silent, love-locked gaze. Her tears began to flow once more. She spoke in a loud whisper. "Bill, I—I've never been in love with a man before. And I--I've never met a man who loves me; I mean one who *really* loves me. All these feelings are all terribly confusing. And wow, they're so *strong*."

Bill smiled with tight lips and a little head nod. He sniffed. "Oh, they're strong."

"But if you really do love me, I'll just ask you to be patient. I've always had to take care of myself, you see, so letting someone else make my choices is awful hard."

Bill grinned. "Oh, it's safe to say I really love you, like forever; and I promise you *every* bit of my patience and understanding."

"My sin was in not trusting you, Bill, and worse, not trusting and obeying God. It was *I* who thought God wanted me in here forever. I now realize He sent you to me. So, does God love me or what?"

Esther took a tissue from the counter, wiped her eyes and blew her nose. She leveled her gaze and her tone. “Look at me. I’m a mess, but just know that from now on, I *do* trust you, and I trust His plan for us as well.”

“Oh my sweet Esther, I still have a lot to learn myself, but this is a road I want to travel *with* you. Together we’ll learn and obey the Lord together.” A guard came up next to Bill and placed a notebook beside him. “What’s this, Esther?”

“It’s my sketchpad for a new book I’m working on. Keep it with the other one.” She glanced up at the ceiling and sighed. “I’ve been praying for the Lord to tell me what to do, and guess what? He did. He woke me up Tuesday morning with four words. I wrote them on the last page of that book. Have a look, Bill.”

His hands were trembling as he opened it up. In large, neat cursive she had written: “Stand by your love”.

“I—I, Esther, what day did you get my letter?”

“Thursday. God gave us those words, that same *command* at exactly the same moment. You wrote it in your letter the *same* time I wrote it on that pad.”

“Oh, wow, you’re right: Tuesday night. That was clever of Him.” He looked up with a grin. “Praise you Lord Jesus.”

"Praise Him indeed, and the message's a blessing too. It also means the Lord is with us."

He grinned. "Then who can stand against us?"

She smiled. "So you *have* been reading Scripture, huh Sweetie? Please know that I do stand in love with the Lord and with you, and I will trust and obey you both."

"Did you say obey?"

Esther giggled. "Yes well, of course in your case, you'll hear my *opinions* too."

"Okay, I'll promise to always ask. I'll also promise to do my best to stay alive. I don't think the mob will try another car bomb, but full precautions will be taken."

"*Hope* so. Now I know what women feel like when their men go off to war."

"Here's the latest on the bomb. They found the boy who planted it under my car. He was given a hundred dollars by someone in a disguise. The man told him it was a stink bomb, just a prank. Same bribe for the college students with back packs."

"Oh phooey, I see our time's about up. A week's *way* too long, darling. You know the schedule when you're allowed to phone. Call me even if there's nothing new. I miss your voice."

"I will, and *you* better get more sleep and start eating, girlfriend. That's an order."

Esther giggled. "Yes, Sir."

ERIK'S ADVICE

Bill stood in front of Myrna's blue-shingled Cape Cod house which was surrounded by live oak and palm trees. He opened the iron gate to the sound of boys throwing a basketball at a backboard over the garage and walked up stone steps to a wooden porch. He was startled by a very deep "woof, woof" from one corner. A huge, long-haired black dog approached him wagging its tail. Bill stood his ground while the Newfoundland gave him the sniff test.

And you are all wet, my friend. He gave him a little behind-the-ears scratch and rang the door chimes. Dog said "woof, woof" again. Bill chuckled. "I think you're only supposed to bark at the bell when you're on the *inside*, buddy."

A tall, lanky man with curly blonde hair answered the door. "Hi. You must be Bill. Welcome. I'm Myrna's husband, Erik."

They shook hands. "Sure am. Thanks for inviting me. Your dog's a bit damp."

Erik grinned. "We have to put Mountain out on the front porch to keep him from having a permanent life in our pool. Lucky he didn't jump on you or we'd owe you a change of clothes."

Erik ushered Bill inside and extended a foot to keep Mountain where he was while he closed the door. "Myrna's in her favorite place, the kitchen. Go in and say 'Hi' while I get you a beer."

Myrna came briskly around the center island wiping hands on her apron as soon as she saw Bill. "We're so glad you could join us for dinner, Bill. You look much better this week. It killed me to see you so depressed."

"I *am* better, and thanks for the invite."

She delivered a brief crunching hug. "Now go on out back and talk with Erik. I'll be out as soon as I get the pie in the oven."

"This is a beautiful place you have, Myrna. In some ways it reminds me more of Connecticut than California."

Myrna began to roll out a pie crust. "Thanks. Our home is all about family fun and comfort."

"You did promise *not* to try and fix me up with someone. I hope you didn't invite me here to meet some lady, did you?"

Myrna chuckled. "Oh, not to worry. I said you didn't need any fixing up, remember? And, besides, I know you already have a special woman."

"I sure do, but she's among the 'untouchables' for the time being."

"Erik might have some thoughts about that. You should ask him."

Her husband was standing in front of a smoking grill near the pool. He raised his spatula when Bill walked up. "Hey, your beer's over by that chair, but first, could you make four more patties for me while I open these hot dogs?"

After a minute they were stretched out on chaise lounge chairs sipping brews and munching peanuts. "So, Bill, Myrna tells me you've only been with her company for six months and I hear you're already in big trouble."

"Is that so? Just what did our 'den mother' report?"

Erik laughed. "Well, let's see. Bad news is you signed up depressed. Good news is she found you some work you like. Bad news is you're gaga over a lady prison inmate and got depressed again. Good news is she brought you to the Lord. Bad news is you started an investigation without her permission. Good news is you actually might be able to get her out. Bad news is the Vegas mob will probably kill you."

Bill stared at Erik, shaking his head. "You know even more than Myrna does. How can that be?"

"I like to think of myself as a triple agent. I work for God, Myrna, and the FBI in that order."

Bill laughed. "Well that explains a lot. Perhaps you can offer some advice on that last bit of bad news."

"Okay, first off, when the police were removing the bomb from under your car, did they find a locator too?"

"Sure did, but it's all gone now."

"Your mobster friends will try and replace it. I'm going to loan you a detector. Keep it in your car and check the reading before you put your key in the ignition."

"Really? Thanks, Erik I..."

Someone shouted and Mountain came bounding out of the house with two boys in hot pursuit. "Sorry, Dad, he barged right in with us." The dog made a huge leap and splashed into the middle of the pool."

"All right boys, close the pet door so he can't get back in." Mountain began to make enthusiastic strokes and swim around in large circles.

"Oh, Dad, Mom said to start the burgers."

Erik got up and looked at Bill. “We’re on duty, but when the dog comes out of the pool stay away from him until he shakes off.”

Bill thought Mountain looked like a monster fur seal as he swam laps around the swimming pool. He noticed an easel on the far side of the pool and the top of a blond head behind it. “Who’s that over there, Erik?”

He chuckled. “Ah, our Bavarian Princess. That’s Linny. She’s also our twelve year old artist. Veggie franks are for her, but don’t be offended if she doesn’t speak to you.”

The Mountain heaved himself out of the pool on the far side, headed for Liny and gave a great water shake off. This was punctuated by a shrill scream.

“Dad! This monster got water over *everything*.”

Erik pointed to a towel draped over a chair. “Bill, would you mind running that over to her.”

He jogged over with the beach towel and noticed Mountain was back at the house, scratching at the pet door. “Here, Linny, I’m Bill.”

She was stamping, shaking her arms and repeating “Oh”. Linny took the towel with a pout. “Thanks. At least someone around here cares. *Look* what he did to my watercolor.”

Bill peered at her picture. "Beautiful seascape, Linny. The water spots make it look like its snowing."

This made her grin and shake her head. "Maybe I'll call it 'Mountain snow scene'. What do you think?"

They both laughed. She handed back the towel, picked up the watercolor and said, "Nice meeting you. I'm taking this inside to dry off in safety."

"Okay, but veggie franks in ten minutes."

Bill returned to the burger-flipping Erik who gave him a quick glance. "Look, Bill, a few more unofficial FBI ideas for you. When you start removing their trackers the goons will be more cautious. Always park in your apartment garage and do the same for work. Both have cameras. Your B.E. guard can help too. Ask him to check the recordings before you leave every day. Get a rental car for whenever you go to go on errands or to your lawyer, and please don't go for long strolls on foot."

"Sounds like I'll be a fugitive for life."

"Nah. Either you'll develop a case or you won't, so one way or another there's an end point."

"Course, if I'm dead, that will be and end point too."

Erik chuckled. "We'll just have to keep you breathing, won't we?"

Myrna came out with a pot of beans and a grin. "Okay everyone, let's eat."

Children came in from all sides and sat at the picnic table. Mountain clumped down under the table by Linny and became a damp, forgiven foot rest.

Myra raised her hands. "Let's pray".

Bill was startled by a hand on each side taking his. Her voice took on a melodious tone. "Dearest Lord, we praise you for making us a happy family showered with blessings. Thank you for this food and for the pleasure of our company today. Thank you for the angel that brought him to the window to look at his car. We ask that you continue to guide and protect our Bill. Amen."

Linny turned to her Dad and whispered. "Protection, Dad? Mom's weird sometimes."

"Oh, nothing, dear. Mother likes to cover all the bases."

After lunch and the best apple pie Bill had ever tasted, Myrna gave him a hug. "Next time you visit, Bill, we hope you'll be able to bring your girl friend. Promise?"

"I'll do my best to keep that one, Myrna."

"We'll hold you to it, you hear? Erik will walk you to your car. He has something for you."

Erik picked up a satchel on the way out to the driveway and sat in the front seat of Bill's car. "Blue sedan across the street's Black Eagle, right?"

"Sure is. Very observant."

"I'm always on the job." He pulled out an electronic device about the size of a large pencil box. "Keep this out of sight in your center console at all times." He flipped on a switch and a green light glowed. "All clear now, but this will pick up any locators. If it flashes red you have one, and the flashes will be more rapid as you approach it. Usually they are under a bumper or a fender."

"Pull it off and smash it?"

"Yeah, fine for the small ones."

"Or hey, I could stick it to a garbage truck. I saw that in a movie."

Erik chuckled. "But, guess what? The mob also adds locators to their car bombs in case they want to wait until the victim drives off. So, if you find something bigger, just walk away and call the police."

"In that case, maybe I'll try running."

"Your choice." Erik reached into the satchel and pulled out a key chain with something the size of a flash drive attached. "Keep this with you at all times. In case of emergency, slide this button forward and squeeze. It activates an FBI emergency beacon and I have the receiver."

"So now I'm an FBI case?"

Erik shook his head. "Not yet, my friend, but if your investigation frees Ms. Green, it will be. This involves known criminals crossing state lines. At that point, we'll be in, your girlfriend will be a witness, and the Service will be much indebted to you both."

THE WARDEN

Flanked by two guards, Esther was escorted down a top floor hall in the Administrative wing. "But why does the Warden want to see me? You never said."

"And we won't. You'll find out soon enough."

They came to a halt before the Warden's door. One gave a quick knock and opened it partway. "We have Ms. Green to see you, Ma'am."

Esther thought the Warden looked like the character she'd seen playing the "Matron of The Orphanage" role in an old movie. She was dressed in a stiff, gray flannel suit and wore her short black hair plastered back against her scalp. The Warden waved off the guards. "We can speak in private. Wait outside."

"So, Ms. Green, why do you think I sent for you?"

"My pardon came through?"

"Why does everyone say that? You know how *tired* that line is? Guess again."

"Ah, you want to know about Jesus."

The warden slammed her palm on the desk and shot up. "Because we still get complaints about you for that sort of thing. Don't you know it's *illegal* to proselytize in here? You've been in solitary for this before. How'd you like it?"

"It was great for prayer and fasting."

She glowered at Esther for a moment. "You know, I don't like your arrogant attitude. You were supposed to be in Yard A, you know, level four with the lifers and other hard ass. I only put you in B 'cause I thought cute-little-you would be *dead* in a week. I ought to put you where you really belong, but I want to teach you something."

Esther was working hard on the sweet, wide-eyed look. "All right, Ms. Green, your free speech right ends when you force yourself on someone else, and that goes for Nancy, too. My right to swing my arm stops at your face, understand? Can't you just preach in the chapel?"

"I do, and I only approach those in need of comfort and understanding. Mostly those women don't come to chapel, and I never pray with someone without their permission."

"Then why am I getting complaints?"

"The women I talk to are not the ones who complain. Onlookers, their former friends and drug suppliers do. They are losing markets and population control."

The Warden's face and body relaxed. "Oh, but she said—well she must have overheard what you were saying. Your words made her uncomfortable and she said she was offended."

"Yes, it's been that way for millennia. For some, repentance and obedience appear to be too high a price. They know surrender to the Lord will be life changing and they fear loss of personal control, even for the prize of eternal life."

"You're not as dumb as you look, Ms. Green. A guard lodged this complaint, so I'm putting you back in Solitary, but just overnight. Tell you what: if you promise not to solicit the unwilling and also explain why this is important to your followers, I promise to investigate future complaints more critically. Understood?"

"Understood, Ma'am. And thank you."

RITA

How can they believe in the one whom
They have not heard, and how can they hear
Without a preacher? How beautiful are the feet of
Those who bring the good news. Ro 9: 14-15

Esther stopped her jog around the exercise yard and peered up into the guard shack. Big Rita appeared to be meditating. Her eyes were closed and her head tilted back, but she sat, humming to herself.

"Ahem, did we have an appointment today?"

Rita swiveled slowly in her chair, looked down on Esther, her eyebrows lowered. "You taking my offer, yes or no."

"No."

She jerked her arm up and pointed to the other side of the yard. "In that case my goodwill ends when you reach that exit door. You want war? You'll get it. *Go*."

"Rita, I'll probably be released this year, and you've called off the beatings. I'll give you what you're asking for free of charge."

Rita's jaw dropped. She stared at Esther, her expression changing while she processed the words. "You're giving up? You do know I might use this mind control thing of yours on your own people."

Esther suppressed a smile. "On my sisters in Christ? Nah, I'm not too worried. Once they've changed it's pretty solid."

"It's that strong, huh? Get up here." She patted the seat next to her. "We won't be disturbed this time. Spill it."

Esther turned the chair so she could face Rita. "I just have one condition and that is you'll first answer any of *my* questions honestly, even if they seem unrelated."

She waved her hand. "No problem, but that goes for *you too*, Greenie. Shoot."

"Do you believe there is a God, a supreme being who rules the universe?"

"Oh, so that's where we're going. You know how to make God do what you *want*, don't you. That's your power over these people?"

Esther covered her smile. 'No, I can't *make* God do anything."

"Oh yeah? What about Adrianna Gomez? She had lung cancer—*both* lungs and spread to the bones. My informant told me you touched her, said some mumbo jumbo and by the time she got back to the hospital—poof, no cancer—none. Explain that."

"You're right I prayed for her, and Adrianna had faith she could be healed, but God does not heal everyone. He acts with wisdom and grace beyond our understanding. Adrianna and two inmates who witnessed her healing came to know the Lord."

"Okay, but how about that crazy one, Missy Stuttgart? You know, talking to herself and shouting at the air. I'm told you did something to her in the Chapel. She screamed so loud four guards came, but when they got there she was acting all sweet and innocent. Still is. That's scary stuff, kid. What happened."

"A demon, Rita, and don't think Nancy and I weren't scared too. But she's one of the sisters now."

"Yeah, and they're *your* sisters now, not mine. But you're saying you can't control God? As I see it, it sure seems like He listens to you. Huh?"

Esther had to chuckle. "Oh, no, He may answer prayers but He is in control of *me*, not the other way around.

But let's back up. I think you answered my first question. You *do* believe in God, don't you?"

Rita nodded her head. "Oh yeah, God's real all right, and don't think I don't know he'll settle up with me in the end, too. But hey, since I'm going to Hell anyway, I'll have a good time while I'm here."

Esther's gaze became direct and searching, and her voice changed to a softer tone. "But, Rita, what if I can offer you a 'Get Out Of Hell Free' card. Are you interested?"

"Don't toy with me, Greenie. You have no idea how big my sins are."

"Hit me with a few."

"Hit you?" Rita pushed a fist into her face but grinned and dropped her arm with a sigh. "Oh, man. I got em all from my ordering murders to selling drugs and girls." Her head fell. "Guess I regret grabbing them girls most. There's some faces I still see at night."

"Rita, can you recall anyone who really loved you?"

"What the hell kind of question is that?"

"You agreed. Any question."

She sniffed and gazed out the window. "Okay, my mother I guess—at least when she wasn't high on something."

"Because you were such a good kid?"

She laughed. “No, I was the *worst.* Ha-ha. Any mother’s nightmare.”

“But mom still loved you.”

“She beat me—but yeah, she still loved me—died last year—cirrhosis and liver cancer.”

“I’m sorry. But Rita, did you know that although you haven’t done much to please God, Jesus still loves you?”

“I seriously doubt that, but back to what you agreed to. What is this power you have to change people?”

“I have no such power myself, Rita, but I lead people to follow the One who does. He changed me and the others. The sisters like each other’s company but we’re not—well maybe from your perspective I guess we *do* look like a gang.”

“You’re still going back to your God thing, aren’t you? He’s not interested in me, so forget it.”

“Well, let’s see about that. In His book He says that we are *all* sinners and sins lead to death. But…”

“Yeah, see what I mean? I’m condemned to death, so I better make the most out of life all on my own.”

“How’s that been working out for you, Rita?”

Rita turned away with a scowl and watched the prisoners jog by.

Esther didn’t interrupt her thinking moment. “But the bible *also* says that *whoever* accepts Jesus will be forgiven of their sins and have eternal life. He died just to make that possible. And, I did say *whoever.*"

"Look, Greenie, why should *you* give a damn if I get religion?"

Esther shook her head with a grin. "Rita, I have prayed for you almost every night. The Spirit tells me that God has a very special work for you, work that will give you redemptive joy. But speaking just for me, I do sincerely care for you and I'm so excited we're finally sitting here talking about Jesus."

Rita turned back from the prison yard. She studied Esther's face. "You do? After what I've done to you?" She closed her eyes. "And you *really* think Jesus would give me a second chance?"

"Rita, my Dear, I absolutely guarantee it."

"But I'd be giving up my power to control people, wouldn't I?"

"The old power of force, yes. But your new boss would be the most powerful person in the universe and you'll know love and joy you never thought possible. You will feel the power of His love, and it will radiate out from you to others as well."

"But what if I don't want to do things His way?"

"If you accept Him, He will write His way on your heart, and you will find that the most joyful thing in your life will be to trust and please the One who loves you."

Rita's voice became hoarse and her eyes filled with water. "Don't toy with me. You can actually take me to a place where I would be loved--and forgiven?"

Esther nodded and gently placed her hand on Rita's ham-like arm. "That's my promise, Rita."

"But what would I have to do?"

"We'll simply begin with a prayer. Will you repeat it after me in your heart and say it out loud?"

Tears had begun to stream over Rita's round cheeks. "Oh, yes."

JAKE

The back corner of the diner had its shades drawn and was dim despite the sunshine outside. Jake was hunched over and kept a wary eye on the door while Bill faced him, coffee cup in hand. "Look, Bill, your guard is a bit too obvious. Why not ask him to use different cars and watch from farther down the street?"

"Okay I will, but listen. This is what I called you for. Esther wants to find out what happened to her friend Ginny who worked in her house in Las Vegas. I'm thinking she could be a character witness, too. Also Lucia, the older woman down the street. Think you can find them?"

He chuckled. "That's how I make a living, Bill."

"Oh, great. She's been so worried about them. Lucia was the one who supported her after she was forced into an abortion. She was like a mother to her."

"I think you said Lucia was the one who taught her about God too."

"More than taught, Jake. They had a real bond together."

"Like a surrogate family, huh?"

He nodded. "Yeah, something like that. She's old, but we still hope she's okay."

Jake took a thoughtful sip of coffee, put down his cup, and squinted out the window. "And there's something you can do to help our case, Bill."

"Just name it."

"I want you to speak to your lawyer. If he'll agree to list me as his employee I can have permission to do a real good search of that evidence room. That missing evidence is the big key to finding the real killer."

"No problem. He wants to have it searched again anyway. I'm sure he'll okay it."

"Well, the problem for me is, I'll have to use my real name."

Bill grinned. "You mean it's really not just Jake?"

"Not funny. I try to avoid any kind of exposure. So listen: here's the deal for me. If I *do* find this all important pouch, how about I get a two grand bonus."

Bill stood and shook his hand. "Deal."

CONFESSION

Alvarez jogged up to Esther while she was walking in a circle around the exercise yard. "Mind if I talk to you Esther?"

"Course not, Maria. You want a salvation prayer?"

(laughs) "Not on your life. I'm Catholic."

"If you're after a spot on Mr. Mason's fall writing class, it's filled up. At this point I couldn't get in myself. Besides, it's in Yard A this time. They won't let him teach here because of our, uh relationship."

"Nah, I just want to come clean with you. I've been spying on you for Jimmy's old organization."

"Really? Who's running things now?"

"Conklin. You're not upset?"

Esther turned to her with a sweet smile. "No, no. It had to be someone and you felt you had no choice, right?"

"Not true. There's always a choice." They walked awhile in silence before Maria resumed. "Things have changed a lot around here recently. Almost everyone is starting to get along. It's real weird."

"Nice weird, or creepy?"

"Strange but nice. It's like someone pulled a plug and let the anger out. And that's saying something with this bunch of prisoners. I know you're a big part of what's happened."

"A great many have found the Lord lately and they're spreading the good news around. Knowing Jesus changes how we look at things. We switch from just focusing on your inside self to looking outward and feeling free."

"Yeah, well, this thing's spread like wildfire." She stopped and stared at Esther intently.

Esther halted also. "What?"

"They wanted me to *kill* you, Esther—snuck in a dose of cyanide. I don't do those things even to people I hate. I'm Catholic, remember."

Esther gently placed her hand on her shoulder. "Thank you, Maria. You took a risk in refusing them, didn't you?"

Maria hugged her and began to sob. "But I *thought* about doing it. Makes me feel real awful when I remember." (sniff) "But, I'll *never* hurt you, Esther, I promise"

A guard spotted them. "Hey, break it up."

Maria pushed away. “Can you ever forgive me?”

Esther’s hand returned to her shoulder. “Already done, and God forgives you too. I just hope the syndicate doesn’t go after you.”

She wiped away tears with her shirt and snuffed. “Nah, I just said it failed. Look, if there’s any favor you need, just ask.”

Esther chuckled. “All right, here’s one. Christian Chapel Service in ten minutes. It’s in the gymnasium this week. Come with me?”

RITA-TWO

Christ was resurrected in the Spirit through whom He went and preached to the spirits in prison.

1 Pet 3: 18-19

Scraping metal chairs sounded out the hollowness of the all-purpose gym as they squeaked over the hardwood floor. The women plucked their chairs from stacks along the side and slid them into rows facing a portable podium. Esther, Nancy and Pacy set up a front row and sat down. Several guards came in as well but they lined their chairs along the side wall.

Esther turned to Maria and gave her a little poke. "Ever been to a non Catholic service before?"

"No, and it sure doesn't look like a church." She pointed to a wooden cross hanging from a folded up basketball net. "There's no one on your cross either."

Esther chuckled. "The one with Him on it is to remember what He did for us, the one without shows He's risen up to Heaven. But guess what? He could come back any time."

Maria turned around to check. "So He's not here to listen to us, huh?"

"His spirit is, Nancy. Don't worry, He'll hear every word you pray."

"Wait, did you see who just walked in?" Maria grabbed Esther's arm with a pinch. "It's Big Rita herself. This yard's getting weirder by the minute."

The prison chaplain walked on stage and the conversation cacophony died slowly as she made her way to the podium. She was a black woman who wore a straight, navy blue dress, a clerical collar and a delightful smile. "Welcome all you daughters of the Lord." She gave them a wave.

She put her Bible down and scanned the audience. "It won't take a government demographic study to see that something amazing has been happening here in Yard B. Just look around you. Not that many months ago fifteen members of our Christian Fellowship were meeting in a small chapel. We had to get permission to move here when we ran out of room, and I'm guessing there are about two hundred saints in here today."

"We got us a full on *revival* here." She raised her arms overhead and looked up. "Praise You Lord for Your *mighty* work. Praise You, Lord Jesus." Her arms came down but her eyes flared. "I hope you all know it's okay to say things like that in here." She cupped an ear and turned it to them. "Well then, let me *have* it."

The audience responded, "Praise You, Lord Jesus."

"Again."

They thundered, "Praise You, Lord Jesus."

"Tell me, that feels *good,* doesn't it?" She chuckled.

"Last time I spoke to you I told you that God loves each of you just as much as Mother Theresa."

Maria whispered to Esther, "But she's a saint."

Esther leaned into her with a grin, "Shhh."

"Well, I've changed my mind. You won't find it in the Bible, but in my opinion God loves the fallen sinner who finds his way back home *even more*. He says the angels rejoice, and I say *rejoice!*"

The Chaplain motioned to two guitar players to set up on the side of the stage. "Okay, but before we begin our regular service I want to introduce—well, on second thought, I guess she needs no introduction. You all know Rita Clough. She has volunteered to say a few words to us." The crowd gasped.

Rita's large form swayed up the side steps and ambled up toward the podium. The chaplain gave her a hug, whispered a few words to her and moved to one side.

Rita's left cheek sported a large purple bruise. She placed her heavily tattooed arm on the podium and leaned forward. "Hey, people, lookie me. I'm in a church."

Rita displayed a wide smile with a missing tooth. "I've had a lot o' firsts the past few months, and standing up here speaking to you guys right now is another one.

"I may still be big, but I'm not 'Big Rita' anymore. And as you can see, some of my former friends don't like me anymore." She chuckled and pointed to her purple cheek. "But here's a sad thing: this body wasn't made for Greenie's ballet moves."

Laughter filled the room and Maria elbowed Esther who's head was down and shaking. "So, I've lost my little 'empire', hardly anyone listens to me anymore, and lots of my old friends hate me. Now I even get the sucker punches I used to hand out. Well, that's justice." She nodded. "Never realized how much they hurt, so if you got one from me before, I'm asking you to forgive me right now."

The room had become stone quiet.

"Here's a message for anyone who'd like to become the old me. Job's open, but right now I am happier than I've ever been in my whole life—punches included." She extended her head forward and squinted. "Yeah, and I see a lot of my old army out there. We all got a *new* boss now, don't we? But don't you go thinking you're hot stuff now just 'cause you got saved and forgiven. We all still got a lot to learn. Don't forget it."

Rita turned to the chaplain who stepped over and put her arm around her shoulders. "Rita has begun to counsel those on drugs and believe me, they *do* listen to her. Anything else you want to say?"

"Yeah." She pointed a finger toward Esther in the front row and waggled it. "That little, *far* too cute woman asked me once if anyone really loved me. Made me think big time cause no one did. I mean, look at me. Who would love *this*?"

She pointed again. "But *that* woman did. She cared. I was the one bashing her face in, and she *cared.* Really made me think."

Esther looked up at her, pure delight on her face.

"In the back of my mind I always knew God was real, but all I could see was His judgment a comin'. See, I assumed I was condemned forever. It never occurred to me that I could be forgiven until she told me.

"Well, I repented and surrendered to Him. Next moment I *know* that Jesus loves me, really loves me. Yeah, *this* ugly old carcass you're a lookin' at. Don't really know *why*, but I'm *so* taking it. He's *God*, you know, and He showed His love when He paid the price for *all* our sins—even..." She shook her head. "Even my pile of garbage."

Rita paused, gripped the podium and looked up. Her voice became raspy. "And I know my list-o-sins is a lot longer than *any* of yours. See, ladies, this changes *everything*. I still got problems a plenty, but once you let God inside of you, you're gonna start being a different person, a better person. And you'll be a happier little camper too."

"Hey, I can't undo all the bad I did to people with selling drugs and stuff, but what I *can* do is start helping one person at a time. Now my life has a *real* purpose—His purpose."

Rita stepped aside, raised an arm and declared a hoarse exclamation: "Praise the Lord!"

The audience responded with a thunderous "Praise the Lord."

Esther jumped to her feet and began clapping above her head. This spread into a standing ovation that spread through the room.

HIDE & SEEK

"Court order given to Reginald Jacobson," the policeman intoned. "All right, Mr. Jacobson, your papers are in order." He shoved them back through the slot. "The judge gave you one hour to search this evidence room, but you do understand I have to be with you at all times. They call you Reggie?"

"Only my mother. I go by Jake."

The sergeant peered at Jake through the steel mesh. "Nice to know you. I'm Jim. Bring your tool box and come around to the security entrance."

"One second, Jim. This little slot for papers—could someone pass an evidence bag through it?"

"Not likely. First, as you see it's only a quarter inch opening, and the electronic sensor on each bag would sound an alarm when it gets close to this window. Besides that, there are cameras on both sides."

Jim met him at the security check and went through Jake's toolbox. Another officer left saying he'd be in the break room. "In addition, when this room's open there's always two of us in here."

Jake looked the room over. "And right now, we're the two guys, huh. So, we're in a basement corner with block walls on two sides and a dropped ceiling. What's above us?"

"Uh, the waiting area and the desk sergeant."

"How about a trap door under the desk up there—a thief coming down on wires in the middle of the night?"

Jim laughed. "What movie was that in?"

"Just funning with you, Jim. Someone is always on duty up there and you have motion detectors in here, right?"

"Of course, and we did a careful check in the area above the drop ceiling. You can look, but I promise you it's clean. The surveillance camera recordings showed nothing suspicious either."

Jake strolled around the room inspecting the rows of compartmented shelves. "Save me some more time. You checked the space between the shelf tops and the ceiling?"

"Sure did. And notice that the *only* shelves that aren't free standing are against the block wall. We also shined a light into every heater duct. That bag just isn't in here, my friend."

Jake stopped and leveled his gaze on Jim. "So what's your theory? How do you think the pouch disappeared?"

"Somebody musta got paid off. Sammy quit the force about that time. I don't know, but I'm just saying."

Jake grinned. "Oh, I agree with you about the bribe, but with this setup it would take three people working together to get it out. You have sensors on the exit doors too."

"I dunno, maybe he wrapped the bag in lead foil."

"Interesting idea. I hadn't thought about that one. But the problem I see is that up to now you've been looking in places where someone would hide something *short* term."

"What do you mean?"

"We need to search in what I call the 'places of eternal disappearance'."

Jake was on a step ladder removing the ceiling fixture. "Like this, for instance."

Next, he tapped along the baseboards with a small hammer and examined the bases of every shelf file. He squinted at Jim. "Do you have to go outside through security every time you go to the bathroom?"

"Oh no, we have one in here." He pointed to a small door beside the exit.

"Just about to ask where that door went. And of course your co-worker goes in with you when you use it."

Jim shook his head with a grin. “Stop pulling my leg.”

“Jim, seriously, that’s the one place where one of you is alone and not on camera. That should have been the first place to look.”

“Knock yourself out. There’s only two vents in there and we checked those. We looked in the toilet reservoir too. Say, you don’t think he flushed it, do you?”

Jake was already on his knees peering into the air return grate. “Can’t flush a revolver, can you? Hand me my Phillips will you?”

He removed the frame and put it to one side. “Look at this. The sheet metal duct has been cut and pushed back in place.” He bent it to one side, reached into his box, and pulled out a flexible tube with a light on one end. “This is kind of like an endoscope but made for a plumber.” He pushed tit through the cut.

“That’s cool. What do you see?”

“Just the inside of the wall—now there’s the top of the duct. No luck.” Jake swiveled it around. “Okay, now I can see the lower part of the wall—I’m moving the scope underneath the air duct—wow! Glory, halleluiah.”

“What? What do you see?”

“I see two thousand bucks. Pass me the pick up tool.”

THE EVIDENCE

Bill squirmed around in Pierce's client chair trying to be patient while his lawyer read and sorted the papers on his desk. "Pierce, it's been over two weeks since I mailed Jake his two grand. Anything useful come out of it?"

He slapped the last paper in place. "There." He greeted Bill with a wide grin. "All good news, Bill, except for Esther. I'll explain."

"The evidence implicates her?"

"Not at all. It points to the real killer, but she'll be a key Federal witness against a prominent underworld figure. She'll need protection on the outside."

"Esther says she feels pretty safe in prison now, but what turned up in the pouch?"

"Lots of new information. The police turned it directly over to the FBI lab for analysis. First, the abrasion on the temple showed rug fiber, and he was found on a tile floor. The blood from his knuckles showed his blood mixed with a man the FBI identified as an employee of the Vegas organization."

"But that doesn't prove he killed him."

"No, but hang on. There was a bloody fingerprint on the deceased's wrist matching the one on the tip of the gun barrel. Note that these were *not* sent to the FBI until now. The prints are from one Isadore Croft, top inner circle in the Vegas mob."

"Wow, that's sounding better."

"The real clincher is the skin under the fingernails. DNA matches Croft as well."

"Better yet, but won't they still say she shot him and they only took her to her car? Her prints were on the trigger."

Pierce nodded. "The missing photos clearly show that the subject was in a fight then bound, hands and feet. And remember, there were no blood spatters at the scene. I have to commend your detective, Jake. He is very good at what he does."

Bill smiled. "He impresses me, too."

"Jake also discovered something remarkable. The department store across the street has a night watchman who witnessed two men matching descriptions of Croft and his employee at three AM. They got out of a car carrying a woman and put her in another car. After that they took a large sack out of their trunk big enough to hold a body, and carried it behind the deceased apartment building. The man also noticed that the police arrived ten minutes later."

"Great! Will he testify?"

"Yes, but even better. He made two copies of the surveillance video. He sent one to the District Attorney when he heard about the trial, and kept the other one."

"But that should have cleared Esther all by itself."

"Right, but there's 'no record' of it being received so it doesn't look good for the former DA either."

"But the good news is we can get Esther out, right?"

"Oh, no question. I'll file the papers tomorrow. For obvious reasons, the FBI are in on the case prosecuting Mr. Croft. They're out looking for him as we speak."

"He's missing?"

"Disappeared the day after Jake found the evidence pouch."

RITA'S RIDE

"Twenty one! I win."

"Aw shoot. Well, I got within three this time, Nancy."

"Of course you're assuming that one serve of mine was really out. Wish they'd let us put some actual lines down on the ground."

They passed the rackets and the shuttlecock to a waiting pair. "I'm grateful the warden let us put this up, Nance. From an anonymous donor last month, huh?"

"Yeah, but who set up the use rules, Esther? I think the winner should be able to keep playing until she's defeated."

They joined the perimeter walkers in the exercise yard. Esther chuckled. "But then no one would ever beat that Indian woman. She'd get to play all day—what's her name?"

"Shanthi."

"Right, the last time I played her she spiked me in the forehead."

Nancy laughed. "Yeah, I remember. She gave you a red mark there just like hers. Uh oh, Big Rita's crooking her finger at you."

Esther gave her a shoulder squeeze. "Okay, see you later."

Rita welcomed her with a hug. "Hi, Esther. Got a minute to talk?"

"We're going to your office?"

"Nah, I got kicked out of my 'Ivory Tower'." She gestured to a corner. "No one's over there."

Esther leaned against the wall. "I'm a bit out of breath still. Nancy makes me run for every shot. You should try and play a game, Rita."

She chuckled. "You'd just *love* to see me try and run, wouldn't you?"

"Badminton's not just about speed. Lots of games are won by those sneaky little dribbles over the net, and I bet your power serve would sizzle."

"I'd learn to play but rumor has it you'll be leaving soon."

"Maybe so, maybe not. My lawyer filed some papers, but we'll just have to wait and see."

"Esther, honey, you're getting out of here. Trust me."

Puzzled, she shook her head. "You know something I don't?"

"I still got my information network, and listen: this old 'tin can' will really miss you. There was meanness everywhere in this yard when you showed up, me being the worst, of course. You could get forked for sitting at the wrong bench for lunch, remember?

She grinned at Esther. "But now—now half the yard is like one big family, and we're softening up the other half. It's all thanks to you."

Esther shook her head. "It's all thanks to Jesus, Rita."

The grin persisted. "I know, I know, but I say you're entitled to a finders fee."

"A finders fee?"

"Yeah, I want to give you something for the good you done me finding Jesus and all. Also something to make up for all those punches you got."

"Rita, seeing you come to know the Lord was sensational. That's more than enough reward for me."

"And I know you mean it, little one, but I'll be real insulted if you don't accept this anyway. You can even give it to charity if you want."

"Probably will, but what?"

"I'm still in here for at least ten more, Esther. I got no use for my mothballed car, but you'll need one soon, so it's yours."

She shook her head. "Oh really, no…"

"No buts. I already signed off on the title. Look, it's not that much. The thing's twelve years old and gets awful mileage thanks to the V8 and bullet proofing, but it's got a kick ass sound system. Anyway, it's yours."

Esther hugged her. "Okay, I accept. That's really sweet of you."

"It'll be at the gate for you when you're released. By the way, when you open the trunk there's a blue button near the latch. It releases a hidden compartment in the lid."

"What's that for?"

"For the heavy weapons, of course." She laughed. "It's empty now but maybe you can use it to pack a picnic lunch for that cute hunk who's nuts over you."

Laughter and hugs.

PRECAUTIONS

Bill walked up to the gate at Erik and Myrna's. Mountain and Linny were playing with a Frisbee in the yard, but the big ball of black hair bounded his way as soon as he went in.

Linny called out, "It's okay. He's dry."

Bill went to his knees to greet him. "But his tongue sure isn't."

She skipped over and ruffled Mountain's fur. "Hi, Mister Mason. Mountain can come inside with us. The pet door's closed."

Myrna and Erik greeted him with a hug and a handshake. Bill protested. "You guys are too good to me, and I've no way to pay you back."

Myrna put her hands on her hips and smirked. "I know, and you're such a *bore*. But this time Erik needs to talk to you about business. Tell you what—just invite us to the wedding and we'll be even."

"Who said anything about a wedding?" Myrna made a crazy face with head shaking.

"And don't forget me." Linny stamped her foot. "I *love* weddings. And I'll paint you a watercolor present, okay?"

Bill had to laugh. "All right, all right, *if* and *when* I get married, you're all invited."

"Good," she said. "So let's eat. You're late and I'm starved."

Dinner conversation was a more conventional discussion of the bad weather back in Connecticut, the boys being away on a camping trip, and Bill's search for a teaching job. Afterward, Erik picked up his pie dish and escorted Bill into his home office.

"Best if no one hears this, Bill." He closed the door and they sat facing each other in soft leather chairs. Erik took a bite of apple pie and set his plate on the desk.

"First, the good news. The judge signed an order this morning releasing Miss. Green with apologies from the state, but for her safety we won't tell her until we work out the release details and a safe place for her. Also, your lawyer is negotiating with California for a settlement.

"The FBI issued a warrant for the arrest of Isadore Croft for murder, kidnapping and conspiracy. We'll find him, but it may take time."

"There's bad news?"

"I'm assigned to witness protection for Esther Green, and she will need it. We are setting up a nearby safe house as we speak, but my first concern is getting her there."

"I sort of assumed you would send an armed convoy."

Erik nodded. "We do that sometimes, but the whole world would know her location, and the press too. Besides, Croft is still on the loose and quite dangerous."

"Oops, I see your point. There's another plan?"

"Yes. All of Esther's papers show her scheduled release a week from Monday, but you have been visiting every Saturday evening. Your arrival the Saturday before with your Black Eagle man is expected by the syndicate. But they won't expect her to be released right then into your custody. Please don't tell her in advance."

"What? Erik, the hair just stood up on the back of my head. You want *me* to protect her?"

Erik chuckled. "Well, I sure hope not. But for this sort of thing, unexpected surprise is the best choice. Of course we'll be moments away if any problems come up. Esther is getting a used car. We've looked it over and we'll deliver it to the release gate."

"I'm feeling pretty nervous about this, Erik."

"And look, you don't have to do this if you don't want to. We can put an agent in the car with her, but if this organization is monitoring anything, it's our activity. You'll have a tracker, but we don't underestimate their resources."

"So, it's supposed to look like my routine visit, and if they don't see the FBI, they won't think she's being released."

"Exactly. Here's the plan. Another prisoner is scheduled for release on the Saturday before. The Warden has agreed to substitute Esther for her at the last minute."

"But, am I supposed to drive her to this safe house?"

"Yes, but you'll just follow your guard. We'll give him the address and route just before you arrive at the prison. And he's armed, of course."

"This is obviously still dangerous, right?"

"It is, Bill. We know the Vegas mob wants our star witness dead, but this is our best plan to keep her alive. The prison isn't as safe as you might think and we believe she's safer under our control. Decide when you're ready. You don't have to do this. We always have a plan B."

"Plan A is prayer, Erik, but I'll do it."

FINAL VISIT

Esther skipped out of the visitation door like a happy child. She kissed her fingers, placed them on the glass and Bill responded in kind. "This is *really* happening, isn't it Bill? I never let myself believe it could."

"Totally real, my Darling. What did Pierce tell you?"

She placed her index finger across her lips. "He's so nice, so concerned. He said not to talk about it, and I actually don't know the day—I think that's on purpose isn't it?"

Bill rolled his eyes to the ceiling. "No talking, huh. Yup, well I guess that's the end of our session." He pretended to be getting up.

"Oh, stop." Esther bounced up and down on her seat and shivered. "I'm just so excited, I can't stand it. I'm only holding back a scream 'cause they'd drag me out again."

Bill laughed and put his hand under the glass. "Soon, my sweet woman, soon."

She put her hand over his, turned her gaze up to the ceiling, bared her teeth and gave a whole-body wiggle. Bill tapped the glass. "But I can tell you some interesting things Jake turned up."

"Really? Did he find Ginny?"

"Jake can find *anybody*, I think. Short story is she married six months ago and is living in Eugene Oregon."

"Oh, that's wonderful. I'm so happy for her. What's the long story? Did he get an address?"

He nodded. "I won't say the address out loud. Did Ginny spend the night at your house sometimes?"

"She did. She was living with this man and felt really guilty about it—wanted to break it off but she was afraid of him. On some nights when he had friends over they'd get drunk and go after her. You know what I mean?"

"I get the picture."

"Well, I set up an attic dormer so she could stay over when she had to. Is this important?"

"Yes, and even you didn't know this, but she was in that dormer when you were abducted--saw you being dragged into a car. She also saw Izzy follow them in your car."

"Oh no. She must feel terrible that she didn't come forward, but of course I understand."

"Yeah, it's no secret she was terrified. She snuck home later so she could walk in and show up for work the next day. Says you told her about a tree route, whatever that means."

Esther giggled. "Oh, that. Go on."

"No one knew what she'd seen. The syndicate discharged all the help that day and put the house up for sale."

"Like they knew I'd never be back."

"Right. Well Ginny took off and lived with a cousin in Oregon. She got a new job and, as I said, she's happily married."

"Oh, that's wonderful. I was worried about her."

"Ginny also said she'd risk coming down and testifying if she had to."

"If they can convict Izzy without her, it would be a lot safer if she stays away, but I'd really love to see her again."

"You will one day, but that's in the 'maybe later' category."

"Any word on grandma Lucia?"

Bill let out a breath and expression drained from his face.

"Uh, oh," she said.

"She passed away over a year ago. I'm sorry. I know you've told me she was the closest thing you had to family."

Esther's head bowed. "She never wrote. Never answered my letters. Was she ill?"

"Here's what Jake found out, and you're not going to like it."

He waited until she made eye contact. "The Vegas mob knew you had spent a lot of time with her. They set up a fake case where Lucia was supposed to have attacked some kid on the street the week after you were taken away. One of their men lived across the street from her."

"I know who you mean. I called him 'police-whistle man.' Scary guy. Hated Lucia's music."

The syndicate made sure she was examined by a psychiatrist who was certainly on their payroll. She was committed to an institution as a danger to others and died in there some months later."

"Oh that's terrible." She covered her mouth. "Poor Lucia. No wonder I never heard from her."

"There's more. Jake discovered that Jimmy's lawyer got himself appointed as guardian with full powers of attorney. They sold or gave away all her possessions including her house. And here's the 'ouch' part. She had left her house to you, but the high powered legal guys got that will dissolved since she'd been declared incompetent."

"But Bill, she had a personal attorney. Don't remember his name, but he must have fought for her. I don't care about the *things*, but maybe she left a note for me or something with him."

"I'll check on that. Pierce could get him to release it if there is one."

Esther put her hand back on the glass so Bill would too. "I want to make this glass go away, my darling."

He sent her an 'air-smooch'. "Soon."

RELEASED

Set me free from my prison that I may

Praise your name. Ps. 142: 7

Stanley, from Black Eagle, had become a familiar face to Bill. He drove Bill through the visitor's entrance, but this time he parked near the release exit so he could watch. He pointed to a car outside the chain link perimeter fence. "That maroon Lincoln is the one Esther is getting. It came in this morning, and we went over it with the FBI. It's clean."

"Big car—could use a paint job."

Stan dropped the keys into Bill's hand. "She'll have her copy of the release papers to show the guard and you two can walk out together through that sliding gate. When you drive out, follow me at a distance."

"Fine, but I have no idea where we'll be going."

"We're headed for a house near San Diego. All you have to do is keep me in sight. After the freeways we'll get off near a park. Rather than take the direct route we'll use the park road to avoid going under any overpasses."

"But no one's supposed to know where we're going."

"An added precaution. You will be in touch with me at all times with the transceiver in your car. Keep about four car lengths back. No closer except at stoplights."

"Will the FBI greet us on arrival?"

"They will be in the house but you won't see them on the outside. "They told me to watch for a gray stucco building. I'm to drive past it and keep going. I'll tell you which one it is on the radio. The garage door will be open and you will simply turn and drive right in.

"Right now you just go in the visitor's gate but keep going past it to the next guard station where you'll hand over your papers. I'll meet you outside. Got it?"

He felt his heart pounding. "What could go wrong?"

"Okay Bill, you're on. I can watch you coming out from where my car's parked."

Bill strode up to the discharge gate, rang the buzzer and tried to relax. Two female guards in flak jackets came outside where he was, but no sign of Esther. Each lifted up a pair of binoculars and studied the surrounding grounds and buildings. Bill imagined a red laser dot at the back of his head and began to feel woozy. *Get a hold of yourself, big guy. Take a deep breath. Esther's coming and you need to be strong.*

One guard squinted at him in the sunlight. "Oh, I know you. You teach a course here. You have the release papers?"

"Right here, Ma'am."

"Where's your vehicle, Mr. Mason?"

"In the lot just outside the gate."

"All right, but one more thing, and it's important."

"Yes?"

She grinned. "Take good care of this woman, hear me? A lot of us in here really love her."

Bill smiled. "Oh I will, I will. I love her too."

She leaned into her shoulder com. "Ready, now."

Esther appeared from a side door in a fluffy print dress and a teased out hair doo. She attempted to walk demurely with her satchel of belongings, but began to run past the laughing guards as soon as she saw Bill. Esther dropped her bag and jumped into his arms almost knocking him over.

They clung to each other raining kisses and tears. Bill could feel the rapid pounding of her heart as they clung together for a moment of sobbing silence. Esther slid down to the ground and began to laugh. "Mister, I sure hope you're ready for all the love that's in this woman of yours."

Bill kissed her gently on the lips and drew her head against his chest. “The paramedics may have to take us to the hospital for detox.”

They were startled by a shout. “Hey you two: *come on*.” It was Stan peering through the gate.

Hands around waists, they walked quickly to the exit. Stan was shaking his head. “Very touching, but standing around in the open is *not* part of the plan.”

He pointed to the vehicle. “Hop in and pull out. I’ll leave when I see you moving. You know what to do, Bill.” He turned and walked briskly away.

Still holding one another, the lovers approached the long, burgundy Lincoln. Bill chuckled. “Black Eagle man. Kinda bossy for his last assignment with me don’t you think? Mind if I drive?”

“You better. My license expired long ago.”

One more kiss before they slid into the leather seats.

Bill grinned. “My, what a big car you have, my dear.”

“The better to snuggle in, my love.”

The engine fired up with a beep bass rumble. “Seriously, now, I better concentrate. Captain says ‘fasten your seat belts’, huh?”

THE EVIL ONE

"Bill, you can put your jazz station back on. If you don't stop me I'll listen to Jesus Rock all day."

"Keep rocking, Dear. I like it too. Besides, you're the one who's been cooped up for three years."

"Okay, but who came up with this plan to get me to the safe house? I expected a bunch of police and FBI guys."

"The Bureau did. They thought a caravan might produce a shootout with the Syndicate, and it would announce your location as well. They had a different inmate scheduled for release when you left to throw any spies off the trail."

"So that's why I got out two days early. But you know nothing is risk free. Izzy's out there somewhere."

"Sure, but the FBI won't be too far away even if something goes wrong. Look, we're finally getting off the freeway. We must be getting close."

Esther turned the music down. "Let's check in with Stan." She picked up the transceiver. "Much farther to go, Stan?"

The speaker responded: "We've got a ways yet. After about six lights I'll be turning right into a small park. Don't loose sight of me."

"Okay, thanks."

A motorcycle buzzed past them. Long brown hair fluttered out beneath the driver's helmet. Stitched around a cross, the jacket back read: "Ride on, King Jesus"

"Oh, Bill, seeing that bike reminds me. Judy Pyle got out three weeks ago. Remember her?"

"Of course. In love with motorcycles, very quiet and apparently unable to smile. However, she's one of the best natural writers I've ever met. Hope she's using all her exceptional talent. You too, by the way."

Esther scrunched in a bit closer and rested her head on Bill's shoulder. "And I hope you'll find a high school in need of an exceptionally talented science teacher."

"Me, too. Ah, there. He's turning off."

They found themselves leaving suburban traffic, following a two lane road that curved through a well-forested park.

The Black Eagle car was only two car lengths ahead when they started to drive down a slope and curve to the right. Stan's voice shouted from the speaker. "Stop right *now*, Bill! Turn around. Go back."

Two vans had pulled out from the bushes on each side blocking the road. Bill panic-stopped to miss Stan and turned around on the road shoulder, but a black limo swerved across the road behind him and slid into his front bumper. Bill's wheels spun in loose gravel when he tried reverse. Trapped.

A man got out of the limo and ran toward them with a pistol held overhead. Esther screamed.

It was Izzy. "Just get out and no one gets hurt." He grinned. "I'm putting you guys on ice until after the trial."

He pulled on the door handle, but Bill had locked it. Izzy waved his pistol at them. "Come on, this is your *one* chance to live."

Esther shouted, "No way, Izzy. Turn yourself in."

"Yeah? How about *this* way." He fired four shots point blank at Esther and Bill.

Bill lay prostrate on top of Esther. "He missed us?"

Izzy stared at the pock marks left on the bullet proof glass and cursed. He looked toward his two accomplices who had Stan handcuffed and shouted, "Quick, bring me the Handy Rifle. Gotta finish this."

Izzy's peripheral vision picked up of a line of motorcycles slowly moving along on the side of the road behind him. They came to a stop. Izzy turned around, flashed a badge and shouted, "Police business. Turn around. Get out of here *right now*!"

One of the bikers thundered back. "Drop your guns, you punks."

"Yeah, says who?"

Stubby shot guns appeared in the hands of every biker. "Says *these*." Fifteen pump loaders slid in unison making a sound like Cloggers stomping out their finale on a wooden stage: "Pah-pum-BUM!" It was a sound Izzy respected.

"Drop em *now!"*

They dropped their guns. Three hefty bikers ran forward, grabbed their weapons and turned Izzy around. They pushed him down on the car hood, and cuffed him. Same for his two accomplices.

Esther and Bill watched open-mouthed as flashing lights appeared from both directions. When the police swarmed over the scene, they dared to get out of their car.

Two FBI agents tried to jerk a reluctant Izzy into walking. He glowered at Esther, his face a bright red. "Esther, you..." He delivered an expletive and spat at her as they dragged him away.

Stan had lost his jacket and came over in a black tee shirt with the company logo on it. "Hey, guys. I'm so sorry. I really thought we had em fooled."

Another agent identified himself to Esther and apologized as well. "I guess you'll get your convoy after all. You know these guys?"

All the bikers were grinning except for one. They leaned on their cycles and slipped their helmets off. She laughed. "Sure do. Mind if I talk to them before we go?"

Esther took Bill's hand and pulled him over to the riders. She embraced two of the women. "Judy, how'd you know?"

Judy Pyle pursed her lips. "If *we* knew, *they* knew."

Mary Stearns bounced on her bike seat, red hair flouncing. "My God, Esther, I was so *scared.* Weren't you?" She jumped off and hugged her. "Thought we were too late. Judy taught me to ride. We didn't have time to get real guns. These are stage props from where I work, and they're made to sound loud. Oh, I'm so glad you're okay. I peed my jeans."

That got her another hug from both of them. Bill was chuckling. "I guess 'glad to see you two again' would be an understatement. And, Judy, is that a *smile* I see?"

"Just realized, Professor," Judy pointed to Stan's shirt. "This was a Black Eagle out on a branch road."

SAFE HOUSE

The small living room had been seething with people, conversations and paperwork. Finally, the local police completed their reports and left, along with the Black Eagle representatives and a small swat team. That left Bill and Esther snuggled on a couch facing Erik and two others from the FBI who remained.

He began, “Look, you two, on behalf of the Bureau I want to repeat our apology.”

“No need, Erik. We totally understand. You did the best you could.”

Esther rested her head on Bill’s shoulder. “Bill was going to take the bullets and save my life.”

“I know, and we all wish he didn’t have to play hero. Truth is we could have done a better job. I had suggested we slip an agent into the car with you, but the team said no.”

"Don't worry about it." Bill pulled Esther closer. "But I have to say, you sure made our first few moments together ones to remember. Just glad they weren't our last."

Esther grinned up at the ceiling. "Bill just loves me something awful, don'cha know."

Erik smiled down on them. "Okay already. I get the picture. Calm down. You're heating up the room. And I really wish I could let you two stay here together, but it's not allowed."

Esther pointed a finger at Bill. "And not allowed by me either." She gave him a doe-eyed stare. "He hasn't even proposed or *anything*."

Bill feigned a pout. "Propose? Wouldn't want to take advantage of my hero status. Maybe later."

She whispered, "You better."

Two female agents stepped up next to them. "Okay, we're here to separate them. Annie, did you bring the crowbar?"

Erik laughed. "Esther, meet agents Annie and Sara. One of them will be with you in this house at all times. They're armed and there will be regular patrols and electronic surveillance outside as well. You'll be allowed to have two dates a week but, sorry to say, there will be agents along for the ride."

Bill shrugged. "Hey, still better than twiddling fingers under a glass once a week."

"Once the trial's over, you can have normal lives again. Good news is that I really feel the danger is past already. Croft is in jail along with his crew, and the Organization from Vegas assumes we already have your deposition. They'll want to distance themselves from Croft and not involve more of their people."

"So no more snipers or bombs?"

"Doubt it, but we'll stay vigilant. I, uh—did the police mention the sniper?"

"No."

"Well, I wasn't going to tell you, but we nabbed one on a gas station roof a few blocks from here."

"Izzy's intelligence info was that good?"

"It was, and that's going to be a separate investigation for us. Someone we trusted had to have given information for a bribe. But, I have another question for you, Esther. How'd you come by a car with bullet proof glass?"

Bill turned to her. "Yeah, and not tell *me* about it, either."

Esther looked up at Bill. "Oh Darling, I completely forgot about that in all the excitement." She faced Erik. "The car was a good luck gift from someone I met in prison."

"I know that part, but who gave it to you?"

"Rita Clough."

Erik stiffened. "Big Rita?"

"Yes, but she just wants to be called plain old Rita now."

"Be honest. Did she try to get you into the LA mob with that gift?"

Esther laughed. "No. The new Rita has become a new creation in Christ."

"Wow. Do you *know* all the things that woman has done?"

"Don't need to, Erik. The past is garbage. It's been dumped behind her forever. She is forgiven by the Lord and, of course, by me as well."

"That's a whole lot of forgiving."

"God has a *whole* lot of forgiveness."

Erik grinned. "You sound like Myrna. And she's dying to meet you by the way."

Sara looked out into the street. "Okay, Erik, if we are done interrogating, Annie and I need to get the kitchen set up. Would you mind picking up the pizza we ordered? I know you're anxious to take Bill home, but these lovebirds have at least earned a little time alone, don't you think?"

TWO WEEKS LATER

Esther bounced through the door. “Hi Annie, I’m home from our date. Great news.”

“I’m in our office room, Esther.”

She dashed in holding her hand up, flashing a ring on her finger. “Guess what? I’m *engaged.*”

Annie stood up, looked at the ring and gasped. “Bling, bling!” She gave her a hug. “Esther, I’m happy for you. I’ve only known you for two weeks, but with what you’ve been through, you deserve it.”

“I knew Bill would ask me, but he made me wait until he found the right ring. Beautiful, isn’t it?”

“It’s gorgeous, girl. But wait, I have to tell you. Erik is coming over soon. He has to explain something about the court case—something important.”

“Pssh, I haven’t paid much attention to that. I just hope the trial’s over soon.”

"But didn't you see the newspapers after Izzy's arrest?"

"No, as I said, I have more important things on my mind right now."

"We save all news reports as part of the investigation. Erik said you should look at them before he arrives. Hold on. They're in the kitchen."

Annie brought them out and they sat on the couch together. "The first one is from a small local paper near the capture point. This came out the same evening as the arrest." She showed her the headline: '*SUSPECTED VEGAS MOBSTER CAPTURED IN PARK, charged with murder. Our reporter on scene*'."

"Sounds about right, Annie."

"Sure, but check our city paper the next morning. It's on page eight, under National News. This one reads like they're reporting on a whole different story. '*NEVADA BUISNESSMAN ARRESTED, Assault charges denied. Attorney promises rapid dismissal*'."

"Almost sounds trivial stated that way. Any follow up?"

"Nada, from any media. Oops, there's the doorbell."

Annie checked the surveillance and let Erik in. "Hey, Erik. Esther's engaged."

Erik's face was grim. He looked at her and let out a breath. "I'm happy for you my dear. We have to talk."

"Why so sad? What's happened?"

Erik pulled over a wooden chair in front of Esther's couch. He sat backward on it facing her. "You checked out the headlines?"

"I did. They're two weeks old."

"Normally the 'attorney promises' thing is just bluster, but as prosecutors we were concerned that all the national papers carried the, let's call it the 'sweet' version."

"So?"

"Today Croft's personal attorney announced who his trial counsel would be. His name is Abraham Wolfowitch."

"Wow, 'The Trial Wolf' himself, huh?"

"Yes. Attorney to the stars, and an almost flawless record of acquittals for those who can afford him."

"But you and my attorney said the case against Izzy is airtight."

"We still think so, Esther, but Wolfowitch declared to the press that he will take this case on pro bono in the name of justice. He requested a speedy trial and the judge gave him one too. It's in less than three weeks."

"But that's great, isn't it? This will all be over soon."

"Esther, these big guys always ask for lengthy postponements to prepare. This means they are *already* prepared. They must have a lot more stuff ready to prove Isadore's innocence--stuff that wasn't needed in your trial."

"Should I say 'uh oh'?"

"Uh oh, indeed. My guess is they will make an effort to dump the crime back on you. I'd suggest you put your attorney on notice, but we won't know anything more about what he's planning until the trial begins."

WOLFOWITCH

In this world you will have trouble. But take heed, I have overcome the world. Jn 16: 23

Agent Sara met Bill at the door. Her usual welcoming smile was missing. She spoke in a whisper. "She's in the work room. I'll be in the kitchen fixing dinner." She walked away but spoke in a hoarse voice. "You're welcome to stay, but she says she's not eating."

Bill stood in the doorway to the small office room. The computer monitor was on, the desk empty. Esther was kneeling on the floor facing away from him, her arms resting on a chair and her hands clasped.

She prayed aloud, "Dearest Lord, in Your great mercy I plead, not just for myself but for the one I love that we might be spared. But in all things I accept and trust Your will, Your purpose for my life. If this is the way things are to be, I ask You to grant me the strength to endure. In Jesus name, Amen."

Esther began weeping into her hands. Bill knelt beside her and slipped his arm around her shoulders. "My God, Esther, what happened at the trial?"

She held him and sobbed into his neck. "It was the first day. It started so, so well, but…." More sobbing. "Oh God, I didn't expect *this*."

Bill produced a tissue and patted at her tears. "But Darling, even if Izzy gets off it won't affect us. Look, I set a date for your plastic surgeon in six weeks and our wedding two months after that. Should be in plenty of time after the end of the trial."

Esther composed herself and they stood up together. Large, sad blue eyes gazed into his. "Cancel everything. I may be going back to jail."

"Okay, look. Let's sit in the living room. Tell me all about this."

Bill grabbed another tissue and sat her down on the couch. "I'm sorry I couldn't be at the trial with you, Esther. You know I had to work, but start from the beginning. You said it began well."

Esther sighed and remained quiet for a moment. "The prosecution's opening statement was very clear, and she spoke well. I felt confident, and you know that Pierce had prepared a Friend of the Court briefing, too. It was Wolfowitch's opening statement that…" Her face scrunched up and Bill drew her gently toward him. "The papers are lying on the floor back in the office. It's the transcript—maybe you better just read it."

Bill went back to the other room and gathered them up. "Is it all right if I read it out loud?"

Esther tossed her hand, "sure".

> "OPENING STATEMENT, DEFENSE
>
> Ladies and gentlemen of the jury, welcome. You will be pleased to know that I do not expect your service will be required for a lengthy trial. This will not be a murder trial at all, but a brief restoration of justice.
>
> That woman I am pointing to has already been tried and convicted of this crime of murder by a jury of her peers and should be still serving her life sentence. At the time of her arrest she was number two in the Las Vegas Syndicate and was known by the nickname, 'Nightshade'. That is a poisonous flower, also known as

'bella donna'. She's beautiful, is she not?

We will prove she personally executed this victim with her henchmen while he was bound and tied at some location in Las Vegas. His body was then transported to his apartment here in California. While the motive at her trial was thought to be scamming, we will present evidence that her true motive was to conceal her betrayal over to the rival Los Angeles Syndicate.

But why, you will ask, was Nightshade released from prison after serving less than three years? Only because new evidence was miraculously discovered, evidence presented by *her employee* to the police. Because of this very act, this so called evidence was obviously manufactured it should be ruled inadmissible in this case. In fact, we will move that her retrial be set aside and this present case be dismissed entirely.

But you will need to know what involvement existed between my client and the murderer. The defense will stipulate that Isadore Croft was Nightshade's, or Esther Green's employee. She called him after the execution and ordered the transportation of the body and he was told to drive her car when she was too intoxicated to drive herself. My client is willing to plead guilty to charges from these actions, but he is innocent of murder.

This trial should not proceed, but if it does, you will need to understand the control this woman has on the people around her—control of so called evidence to frame my client, and even control a manufactured incident where they accosted him, put him in handcuffs, and presented him to the police.

> During the first years of her well-deserved incarceration, Nightshade worked her prison yard like a Community Organizer. She recruited half her yard into an organization and, not surprisingly, many were recruited from the Los Angeles Syndicate. It is uncontested that upon her release from prison, a top officer of that group presented her with a limousine—a *bullet proof* limousine, her new staff car.
>
> So in conclusion, the defense will request that all charges against Isadore Croft be dropped and this trial be dismissed."

Bill fell into the couch beside Esther and dropped the papers. "Wow, I see why you're upset. But this is all a lying fabrication. What happened next?"

Esther's head was bowed and she spoke softly. "The judge called the lawyers forward, talked to them privately and then announced that he would consider the petition in chambers. He ended the trial until tomorrow morning."

"But, Esther, they can't put you back in jail. That would be double jeopardy, wouldn't it? What did Pierce tell you?"

"That it's a tricky call. The Wolf said the Court wouldn't be retrying me, just cancelling my release documents. Pierce said he'd review past rulings."

"Can I help?"

"You can. Let's pray together—right now."

OPTIONS

Pierce had requested an evening meeting with Bill and Jake to review the disastrous turn the trial had taken. They gathered in Myrna and Erik's living room.

"Let me just say one thing completely off the record." Pierce took a sip of lemon water and placed it on the coffee table. "I hate this guy. He's why our profession has a bad reputation." A quick toss of the hands. "But, as you can see, he's also a real tour de force."

Jake chuckled. "And full of more lies and deceptions than the Devil himself."

"True, but notice how some of his lies are based on smidgeons of truth. By the way, the prosecution has authorized me to act as a co-council."

Myrna humphed. "It's just disgusting. He should be sued for libel—oh, and there's fresh coffee if you want some. And you won't like it, but here's today's paper."

The front page read: "Murder trial for Nevada businessman may be dismissed. 'Evidence' against him was delivered by employees of the convicted murderer. Judge to rule tomorrow."

Pierce pointed at Jake. "Forget that. You said you had something for us?"

"Not directly about the case, but you remember Wolfowitch's press release about taking this case pro bono? Piqued my curiosity, so I researched something all on my own." He chuckled. "And *my* report really is pro bono."

"Wolfowitch, otherwise known as the 'W', is CEO of 'Legal Practicum', a high profile tax exempt foundation with a heart rending Mission Statement. Basically it does do a tiny bit of work for the poor, but mainly it covers up a money funnel to Wolfowitch.

"Last year Legal Practicum expanded to a high rise in downtown San Diego and left its four story office near the airport. The day after Croft's arrest, JB construction from Las Vegas bought the smaller building."

"Yeah, but that's just a favor," Bill shrugged. "Nothing really illegal about that, right?"

"Bill, the building has an assessed value of two point five million. JB paid twenty four million for it."

Pierce laughed. "Nice retainer, huh? But it won't help our case."

Jake shrugged. "I know, but that's how things work in the big city. It's likely the press won't even cover it, but I'm leaking it to a Wall Street Journal reporter I know."

Erik spread his arms. "Look, Monica Smith is one of our best prosecutors and I'm confident her team will dismantle every lie one by one, but the W has put us on defense. Fact is, if the judge rules against the bag of evidence, we'll lose the case. Right, Pierce?"

"Oh that's probably true, but I can't see him making a decision like that all on his own. We have Officer James ready to testify he saw the pouch come out of the wall."

Myrna saw Bill's head drop. "Bill, how is dear Esther bearing up under all this?"

"She was devastated at first, but it scares me how tough she can be. She really believes if she's going back to prison, it's God's will."

"Well, I'm sure it's not, but bless her for trusting Him." She frowned at Pierce. "They can't *really* send her back, can they?"

"I don't think so. Well, it would be a stretch if they did."

"You don't *think* so?"

"I can't be positive. The hearing that freed her should protect her under the double jeopardy clause. But if that evidence were shown to be deliberately faked as W alleges, we just might have a problem. My staff is working on that right now."

Erik said, "But we all know it *is* genuine."

"Of course, and I think we can prove that it is. Look, most of what Wolfowitch is doing is building doubt in the minds of the jurors. He just needs reasonable doubt to get his client free. For instance, the night watchman's testimony—the man can't actually identify the people he saw. The W will chew him up on the stand."

Bill slapped his hand on the arm of the couch. "Okay Pierce, let's have it. What is the worst case scenario we're facing?"

"Worst case? That the judge would disallow the evidence pouch. He won't stop Croft's trial, but he might ask a higher court to review the validity of Esther's release trial. We could lose both trials."

Bill slumped back. "That's a good worst case. It beats out the huge meteor destroying the Earth thing."

FIRST WITNESS

What is truth? (Pontius Pilate, 33 AD. Jn 18: 38

Judge: "I have ruled that this trial will continue, but we will first hear witnesses concerning this evidence pouch."

The W called the first witness. "State your name and occupation, please."

"Myron Rogers, detective, San Diego Police Department."

"Thank you. Myron, do you know the defendant, his family or anyone who works at JB builders?"

"I do not."

"And having been sworn in, may we assume your answers will be true and correct even if they may cast another police department in a bad light?"

"Of course."

"Good. The bailiff is bringing you an evidence container typical of those used in San Bernardino County. Detective Rogers, does this look familiar to you?"

"Sure. It's similar if not identical to the ones we use."

"Can you pull off the label and the bar code for us?"

Myron did so and held it up. "All right, Myron, stick it back on. "Do you think it's possible to switch labels on evidence bags like these?"

"Sure, but that would be a criminal offense."

Wolfowitch grinned at the jury. "Yes it would be, Myron. And do you see the photo of the bag in question?"

"Yes, Sir."

"In your expert opinion, is there anything different about the plastic bag in the photo and the one in your hand?"

"Well, it looks whiter and not so transparent. Also the sticker may not be on straight."

"So, would you say that it's probable this was a substitute bag and a hastily applied ID label?"

"Well, I guess—at least it's possible."

"Thank you for your expert opinion. No more questions."

Judge: "Does prosecution wish to cross examine?"

"Not at this time, your Honor, but we reserve the right to recall. If Defense has no more witnesses on this subject, we would like to call our first witness."

Judge: "You may."

Monica gestured to a man near their table. “We call Officer James Oletsky of the San Bernardo Police Force.”

He was seated and sworn in. “Officer Oletsky, how long have you served on the police force and how much of it was in the evidence room?”

“Twelve years in the force, seven at San Bernardino, and almost three years with evidence room detail.”

“So it’s safe to say you are very familiar with evidence security at your station.”

“Yes, Ma’am.”

“Tell us what you know about this special pouch.”

“This was the evidence collected for the Esther Green trial. Uh, she was Esther Braugh then.”

“Jimmy Braugh’s wife from Las Vegas?”

“Yes. At that time Sammy Coletti was one of the officers assigned to the room, and he was still there when we looked for the missing pouch. He’s retired now.”

“So the evidence pouch disappeared before Esther’s trial?”

“Yes M’am. We looked hard for it, too. I was Sammy’s replacement as officer in charge when he left.”

“But the bag was later found. Tell us about that.”

“Sure. Esther’s lawyer hired a private detective to do another search. I was with him all the time of course. He found it hidden inside the bathroom wall. That was a real clever hiding place. I was impressed."

"And how did you identify this as the missing evidence?"

"Well, first I took a picture of it, checked the bar code, and I called my supervisor. We opened it together, verified the ID and the contents against the recorded inventory. It was the missing evidence all right."

"I have no more questions." Monica turned to Wolfowitch. "Your witness."

Wolfowitch rose slowly and began a thoughtful paceing in front of the jury. He faced the jury and gave them the smile of beatific patience. Still looking at them, he addressed the witness. "Mr. Oletsky, we would like to first ascertain your confidence level that the pouch this man Jake handed you was indeed the *untouched*, original evidence bag."

He took two brisk strides toward the stand. "Would you say you were confident, pretty sure, or probably sure?"

"I'm confident, Sir."

The W spun around, flashed a surprised look to the jury, and turned back to Oletsky. "Really? How could you be *certain* that Jake didn't have other materials in his pockets?"

"Whether or not he did, the bag we retrieved was sealed."

"And just what is the seal on this evidence pouch?"

"They're Zip Lock bags, sir."

Wolfowitch half turned toward the jury, his eyes rolled up and his expression whimsical. "Ah, waterproof, and such *tight* security, too. Why do you think this bag was white, and the others clear?"

"It was covered with white drywall plaster dust when I took the photo, but it had the same bar code as the original bag."

"You know, I'm inclined to *agree* with you." He held up a cautionary finger to the enraptured, open-mouthed jury. "Officer Stanley, how long have you known Jake?"

"First time I met him was the day he came to search."

"So no one told you that in college he entertained his fraternity brothers with slight of hand magic tricks?"

Stanley shook his head. "I see. Did Jake put his hand in the wall before he retrieved the pouch?"

"Maybe a little."

"Maybe a little. Could you see *all* of his hand *all* of the time?"

"He used his fingers to bend out the metal duct, but then he used a retrieval tool to pull out the sack."

"All of his hands, *all* the time?"

"Mostly—except for his fingers."

"Mostly—except for his fingers, his slight of hand, magic-trick fingers." Wolfowitch turned to the judge. "Well I think no more questions are needed."

Judge: "Counselors please approach the bench." They came up and stood. "I have listened to the statements these witnesses have made and I will allow the contents of the evidence pouch to be used in this trial." The Wolf gave the jury a look of pain and shock.

"You may of course challenge each piece of evidence separately on its own merits, and you are free to examine them and their associated reports. I will allow you until tomorrow to do so unless you request more time. Court is adjourned."

Pierce turned to Esther. "Well that's good news at least, but tomorrow we're on. I think we should do a little preparation at your safehouse, say after supper at seven?"

COUNSELOR'S PLAN

Esther's arm rested on Bill's shoulder as they sat at the kitchen table. Pierce grinned. "You are looking much better my Dear."

"I'm guessing I won't be going back to prison." She tilted her head and batted her eyelashes.

"No way. You're safe. With that evidence bag in the trial, no matter what the Wolf does to individual pieces of evidence, you can't be tried again. The W may still talk about it in court, but that'll be just for jury hype."

Bill turned and kissed her cheek. She kissed back. Pierce chuckled. "Okay you two, we have work to do."

Pierce slid papers across the table. "Transcript copies for your records. Just so you all know, I've pushed back my entire schedule to be part of this case."

Esther's eyebrows dropped. "Oh Pierce, if there is someone more deserving, we'll manage."

Pierce chuckled. "No need to play Mother Theresa. My signing on isn't just altruism. A chance to go up against Wolfowitch makes this a dream case for me, and Monica is pumped, too. I expect reporters will be poking microphones at you asking you questions coming and going. Just smile and say you're not allowed to comment."

Bill flopped a newspaper on the table. "We're on the first page. Did you see this?"

Pierce shook his head. "Better to just ignore what they're saying."

"Really? But suppose the jury got a look at this. I know they're not supposed to, but listen to these quotes: "Prosecution alleges the defendant, Mister Croft, has underworld connections, but offers no proof. Person working for the previously convicted killer delivered the 'so-called' new evidence against him."

He slapped the paper. "Esther should be allowed to tell the true story—all of it, don't you think?"

"Okay, here's the thing. The Wolf will expect us to do just that. He'll deride it sentence by sentence and ask the judge to instruct her to answer questions only. Here's what we'll do instead. Monica will lead with Croft's henchman and put some initial holes in your character assassination. Next, I'll put you on, Esther, but this time it will be short and sweet. Just give brief simple answers. On cross he'll try and break those down, but I'm betting he'll resume with an attack on your character. He thinks that's his strong suit."

"You want him to?"

"Oh yes, because then I can appeal to the judge to allow you a full *narrative* by way of defense. Believe me, your *real* story will melt every juror's heart."

Esther nodded. "Whatever you say, but why is Wolfowitch so mean?"

"It's actually not meanness. He knows that Croft is guilty, so his plan is to befuddle and raise doubts about you, the evidence—everything. But I'm impressed by how calm you've become. Why is that?"

Esther grinned. "After the trial we should talk about that, all right?"

TRIAL DAY THREE

Monica called out: "I summon Sidney Jones to the stand, please."

A broad shouldered, lanky man ascended to the witness chair in gangly, twitchy movements.

"Mister Jones, who is your employer?"

"Izzy, Ma'am."

He looked at Izzy who was making faces at him. "I, well, actually JB Construction. Yeah, my paycheck says JB Construction."

"All right, but your immediate boss is Isadore Croft, is it not?" He nodded. "Let the record show he nodded in affirmation."

Monica moved in closer carefully blocking his line of sight to Izzy and the W. "And who is *Mr. Croft's* boss, Sidney?"

"I, uh, I'm not supposed to say." There was a murmur of laughter in the court room.

He peered around Monica. "Oh, I don't really know. That's it."

"Sidney, it's all right. You're under oath and it can't really be a secret, can it?"

"Uh, no I guess not. It's Mr. Conklin."

"That would be Benjamin Conklin, present owner of JB Construction, correct?"

"Yeah, that's right."

"But at the time of the murder it was someone else, right?"

"Yeah, well Jimmy Brough ran everything then, but he's dead."

"Killed in a shootout at a narcotics bust, correct?"

"I, uh…" He craned around trying to see Izzy. "I—that's what the *papers* said,"

Monica gave him a moment. "It's all right, Sidney. Did you know Esther Green back then?"

"Sure, she used to be his wife, Jimmy's I mean, before the divorce."

Monica moved in as close as she could, smiled and spoke softly. "Sidney, I want you to think back. What was the nickname they used to call Jimmy's wife?"

His face went blank. "I, uh—there was a nickname?"

"Yes, something else people might have called her—like your lawyer is sometimes called 'The Wolf' by the press." Murmuring laughter.

"Oh yeah, we sometimes called her 'Miss Sweetie' cause she was so cute and nice to everyone. But usually we only saw her at public parties and stuff like that."

"And did 'Miss. Sweetie' ever boss people around? You know, give you any orders?"

"Oh yeah, she bossed me once big time."

Monica jerked back. "She did? What was that about?"

"One time she ordered me out of a JB party."

"She *ordered* you Sidney? Why was that?"

"I was working at the party and passing a plate of those snack things around. She said I couldn't come back until I washed my hands."

"I see." Monica covered her mouth and waited for the giggles in the jury to die down. "But getting back to this *murder,* did you have anything to do with it?"

"Nah, nuttin. That was the other guys."

"What other guys, Sidney?"

His look became desperate, furtively glancing around the defense table. "Some other guys. I dunno." He pointed to Esther. "They said it was *that* dame. I wasn't there."

"Really. Miss. Sweetie? But what if we showed you evidence that you contacted the body?"

"Oh no, the creep was dead when I got there. Izzy just called me to help move the body."

"Where to?"

"From the alley behind Bennie's Bar to some place in San Bernardino."

"And was Esther there?"

"I, uh, don't remember."

"Really? I would think you'd remember if Miss. Sweetie were there."

"She was—uh--I don't remember."

"At least you're sure she was in Las Vegas, right?"

"Yeah, in her house, but I don't remember."

"Sidney, you were remembering so well. What happened?"

"They told me to say I don't remember." Subdued audience laughter.

"*They* told you…"Monica stepped aside and gestured toward the defendant's table. "Those guys?"

A lawyer at the table rose up. "I object. She's leading the witness."

Monica grinned at the judge. "That's okay, your Honor. No further questions."

When she returned to the prosecution table, Pierce whispered to Monica. “Pretend you just got a high five.”

On cross examination Wolfowitch spent his time “clarifying” Sidney’s memory about how he couldn’t be *certain* that Esther hadn’t been there, and that Esther *might* have been the one asking Izzy to move the body. Also, he didn’t really know her well enough to hear of her nicknames.

ESTHER ON THE DOCK

The court was in recess for lunch, and Pierce, Esther and Monica sat at a corner restaurant table with support staff. Pierce gestured to Monica, opening his hands. “You know, that wasn’t as bad as I expected with our security guard. His video did prove that Esther was carried by two men to her car.”

Monica slung her long black hair over one shoulder and took a bite of her tuna sandwich. “Yeah, but what’s that really prove? Their new line is she killed the victim in Vegas and got stoned after she got to San Bernardino.”

“But if they worked for her, why wouldn’t they have driven her back to Vegas? Also, I like the part where you noticed those little puffs of smoke from one guy’s hand. Had to be purposeful shots in the air made so witnesses would say they heard them.”

"Thanks, but again no one is contesting the body wasn't moved to his apartment. Who ordered it and who shot him is the only thing that matters."

"You're right, but are you sure you're okay with my asking Esther the questions this afternoon?"

Monica nodded. "Absolutely. You've worked out a good approach with her and she's comfortable with you."

"Yeah, but let's hope we don't hear any more jury laughter with W's facial expressions." He turned to Esther. "Remember, it's okay to show emotion when he insults you and your statements. You're a tough cookie, Esther, but today I want to see your vulnerable side. When Wolfowitch attacks I want you to be 'Miss. Sweetie' again."

With Esther seated in the witness chair, the Bailiff strode over with a Bible in one hand and held it out to her. "Do you, Esther Green, solemnly swear or affirm that what you are about to say is the whole truth and nothing but the truth."

Esther reached out and gingerly stroked the book. "Oh, it's a King James. I will not swear, but my yes will be yes and my no will be no. I will speak only the truth."

The Bailiff scowled at her and turned to the recorder. "She affirms."

Pierce was suppressing a smile as he approached Esther. "Good afternoon, Miss. Green. Let's not waste the jury's time. Please introduce yourself and explain your situation at the time of the murder.

"I was eighteen and foolish when I married Jimmy Braugh five years ago. Rather than live with me, he kept me away from himself and his business. My function, so to speak, was to accompany him in public. He kept me in the dark about his business, but when I realized there were probably illegal components to it, it was too late. I knew he had lied to me about his business and loving me, but I was afraid to try and leave him.

Pierce nodded. "And recount for us the events of June sixth, two-thousand eleven, the night of the murder and your arrest."

"Sure. I was at the Las Vegas house Jimmy Braugh kept me in. It was almost ten o'clock, and I was alone and starting to get ready for bed. I heard people talking outside the front door and came downstairs to see who it was. Isadore Croft came in with two people. He was one of Jimmy's associates. Izzy had the key, but he's supposed to ring the doorbell."

"Did you know the men who were with him?"

"Vaguely—well one of them anyway." She pointed at Sidney. "One was that man, Sidney, but the other one I'd never seen before. He was carrying a doctor type bag but he didn't look like a doctor except he had a face mask on."

"Anything more about him?"

"He was wearing a black jogging suit. He had black curly hair with grease in it, and mean eyes."

"And what was the first thing Izzy said to you?"

She made a 'humph', and looked up in thought. "No one asked that before. Let's see. Oh yes, Izzy said 'Your so lucky. You're getting a free sample, courtesy of Jimmy. You're gonna love it,' or something like that."

"He meant a shot of drugs like those sold on the streets by Jimmy Braugh's network, correct?"

"Objection, your Honor." An assistant attorney on defense was standing with one arm upraised. "Leading the witness and accusatory."

Judge: "Sustained. Rephrase."

"A sample of what, Miss. Green?"

"Clearly some drug cocktail. I screamed at them to get out of the house and leave me alone."

"Izzy said 'We can either do this the easy way or the hard way.' I said '*hard* way', and tried to run."

She looked at Izzy who sat nodding and smirking. "They caught me, gagged me and held me down. Izzy sat on my legs and Sidney held one arm and my hair. The stranger took a needle out of his bag and gave me a shot in my other arm."

Esther's head was down and shaking. "I'm sorry, Miss. Green. We understand. Take your time."

"It's all right, Sir, but I was so scared. I don't like to think about it."

"Understandable. What happened next?"

"The next thing I remember is being in my car and people shouting for me to get out. Their voices sounded garbled and far away."

"These were the police?"

"Yes, but I was so woozy, all I could do was open my eyes. I heard glass breaking and they were pulling me out."

"And the police arrested you."

"Yes. When I woke up I was in San Bernardino. I guess the rest is a matter of record."

"It is, and I thank you for your time, Miss. Green." Pierce turned to the Defense Table. "Your witness."

Wolfowitch had a smooth swagger of a walk as he approached Esther. "That was such a touching story, Miss. Green. Did you use it when you were on trial the first time?"

"No, they didn't put me on the stand, but a policeman witness told them about finding me in the car."

"And they still convicted you of murder. Why do you think that happened?"

Pierce called out, "Objection. Asks for speculation."

Judge: "Sustained."

"Miss Green, please tell the Court about your first arrest for drug possession."

"I, I never used drugs. I was never arrested before."

"Miss Green, you know that is not true. May I remind you that you are under oath and lying has penalties." He stood, smirking at her furrowed brow. "Let me help you remember. You were a high school senior and police found drugs above your locker."

"Oh, that." Esther chuckled. "The police questioned twenty two of us with lockers on that side. Whoever had the bag of weed tossed it on top of the lockers and their dog found it. He was a cute white Lab named Bo. Our 'arrest' was really just a stern lecture to all of us in the gym."

"Did you know the bag was found above locker 112? That was *your* locker, Miss Green."

She pouted at him. "They never told me, and I never used the stuff. You ever try weed, Mr. Wolf?" Snickers were heard in the audience.

“The second time you were caught they dragged you out of a charity ball on a cocaine charge and put you in a police car. I’m sure you remember *that* one, don’t you?”

“Sure do. My limo driver had lit up in the alley. He was waiting for me to leave. The police called me out for questioning.”

“Questioning because the man claimed you gave it to him.”

“Oh yes, that’s right. And a police woman searched my cocktail dress and my clutch purse. They had a dog sniff the purse too. He was a German Shepherd and not real friendly, but the nice police woman apologized and offered to drive me home.”

“Would you deny that your husband was running the Las Vegas Drug Syndicate?”

“I would not deny or accuse him either. His involvement was widely reported but I had nothing to do with any of the businesses he ran.”

“I see. Also it was widely reported and you had evaded two charges of drug use. Yet you would have us believe you married a man involved with drugs but didn’t know that?”

“Yes sir. I really thought he was just a building contractor. That’s what all the papers said, too.”

"Really. Would you deny that anyone in his organization would have easy access to drugs?"

"No."

"And wouldn't Jimmy's wife have first choice?"

Pierce stood up. "Okay, that's enough. Badgering the witness. Is there a point here?"

Judge: "Counselor?"

W: "The use of drugs is linked to the moment of her arrest. I address her character and probable use at the time of the murder for which my client stands accused."

Judge: "Overruled."

Esther glanced from the judge to the attorneys. "Oh, okay. Jimmy kept his wife, that was me, on a strict set of rules, but I wouldn't have taken any of his drugs even if he let me. Truth is, I don't think Jimmy was a user himself."

"Miss Green, would you deny that on the night of the murder you resorted to using drugs anyway? Killing someone can be a very upsetting thing, can't it?"

"Not using but they were in my system. I told you how they got there."

"Would you deny that you had the track marks of a habitual user on both of your arms?"

"They weren't there earlier that day."

"Really?"

"Really."

"Miss Green, what is your opinion of the defendant, Isadore Croft?"

"I pray daily for the salvation of his eternal soul." Audience tittering.

"Oh, that's very cute—a nice way to accuse him of a crime he didn't commit. But you know who murdered this man, don't you?"

Esther calmly looked into Wolfowitch's blazing eyes. "Sir, among all your witnesses, I was the one asleep and under full anesthesia."

"So you say, but you do not have one shred of real evidence to prove you were under the influence of drugs *before* the murder, do you?"

"You have my word of truth."

"Do you deny that the victim was shot with *your* gun, with *your* fingerprints on it, and it was found in *your* possession near the murder scene?"

"They set me up pretty good, didn't they?"

"No one believes you were under anesthesia when you fired that gun."

"Objection! Unfounded accusation."

Judge: "Sustained."

"No further questions at this time, your Honor." Wolfowitch strode briskly to his seat and thumped down.

Judge: "Redirect?"

Pierce said, "I don't think so. Not at this time." He motioned Esther back to their table.

Esther slid in between Monica and Pierce. "But I thought your plan was to shore up my character or something like that."

"Changed my mind. Your character speaks with profound eloquence for itself. The Wolf still has the element of doubt he wants, but right now he's not real happy."

Monica's assistant came up from behind and spoke softly. "There's someone in the audience who says she is a witness."

Monica stood and was recognized. "Your Honor, may we have a short recess. We may have one more witness to introduce today."

Judge. "Granted, ten minutes."

MRS GARCIA

Esther turned to see who was coming down the aisle with the bailiff. She was startled to see a familiar Hispanic woman in a print dress, her black hair loosely gathered back from her face with a head band. “Ginny!” The two friends embraced. “Pierce, this is Ginny, my best friend in the whole world.”

Pierce took her hand. “The same Ginny who Jake told us about?”

“Oh, yes sir.” She grabbed Esther’s shoulders and embraced her again. “I am so sorry I not come down the first time, Esther. I thought they were killing you, and I was scared, so I run. Then I hear you in jail. I think I can do nothing.”

Pierce turned to Monica. “This is what answered prayers look like, my Dear. This woman witnessed the abduction.”

Her eyes widened. "Wow. You go ahead and put her on."

"I'd love to but this time my sense is it would be better if it's woman to woman. Enjoy."

Monica glanced at the defendant's table where Izzy was standing, pointing at Ginny and arguing with Wolfowitch. "Looks like *they* know who she is, Pierce."

Monica stood to one side so the jury could see their new witness clearly. She smiled. "Please state your name and occupation for the jury."

"My name is Virginia Alonzo Garcia. I work for Happy Housemaids. They in Eugene Oregon."

"And what was your position at the time of this murder?"

"Then I work for Misses Rogers Housecleaning. That in Las Vegas. They put me full-time working in Mister Braugh's house. Maybe I work two years there."

"What was it like working for Mister Braugh? Did you get along?"

"It was easy house to clean. Only Esther live there. I only see Mister Braugh two, three times. Martha was cook and she in charge mostly."

"But, help me understand—may I call you Ginny?"

"Of course, Ms."

"And please call me Monica. I thought Esther was married to Mr. Braugh."

"Yes, Ms Monica, but she only a wife for special occasions, to show to others."

"A trophy wife?"

"Yes, that what you call it. She was very lonely and not allowed to go out much. Martha watch her and Izzy tell her on phone what she must do."

Monica stood up straight. "Wait, are you referring to the defendant, Isadore Croft?" She gestured in his direction. Izzy's face mimicked Ivan the Terrible.

"Oh yes, Monica. Esther only allowed to go shopping twice and to church one time a week. Izzy say she not allowed to have friends visit. See, that why she so lonely."

Monica looked at the jury. "I can think of other emotions a woman might have besides being lonely." She turned back to Ginny. "But how did you two get along?"

She grinned at Esther. "Oh, we are good friends, I think. Esther helped me with the housework and sometimes Ester say she not hungry so cook go home for lunch. Those times she would take me out to restaurant. Cook not know we went out."

Monica shook her head. "Oh, that sounds so *sinister*. Glad you weren't caught. Did Esther have any other friends?"

Wolfowitch stood up. "Objection, your Honor. Where is this leading?"

The judge gestured to Monica. "Counselor?"

"The activities of the defendant relate to Esther and her friends who knew the defendant. Will the Court bear with me for a moment longer?"

"Go on then."

"Ginny, did Esther have any other friends?"

Ginny squirmed in her seat and stroked her hair back before she answered. "She good friends with Grandma Lucia. She live down the street. They meet after Mister Brough make Esther have abortion."

"Whoa!" Monica spun completely around and clamped her hands on the witness table. "What? *Who* made Esther have an abortion?"

Wolfowitch himself jumped up. "Objection your Honor. We are now far afield and probing hearsay not related to this case."

Judge: "Counselor?"

"On the contrary, Esther's disobedience to Mister Brough in trying to have a child was central to the motivation for her being framed for this murder."

Judge: "All right, but relevance must be made clear." He faced the W. "You will be able to examine any statements on cross."

Monica sighed and spoke softly to Ginny. "All right, Ginny, tell us about the forced abortion."

"She supposed to take the pills. Cook Martha check on her, but Esther want a baby so she spit them out when she not looking."

"So she became pregnant. What happened?"

"Izzy and two men drove in garage and sent me and cook home. My car down the street, but I come back when I hear her scream."

"Esther?"

"Yes. Front gate open so I go to side. I look in window. Izzy and the men holding her down. Then they carry her to car. She come back later--a few days. No more baby. She very sad—very, very sad."

"I think we all understand, Ginny. How did this relate to Grandma Lucia?"

"After that, Esther start to walk around neighborhood. She not supposed to do that either. Cook Martha mad. So was husband and Izzy when they found out. But she met Lucia. She down the street. Lucia tell her a lot about God, and she felt better again."

"Good. So she was getting back to her old self ?"

"Oh no, Ms Monica, she different self I think. She got to be with God then, and she tell me about Him too. Before I think religion was church, but now I know it *inside* of you. It is Jesus and the Spirit." She patted her chest. "In here, you see?"

"I'm not sure I do, Ginny, but just so we don't get another objection from the defense table, how long was this before the murder?"

"Six, maybe seven months."

"Okay, what do you know about the night of the murder?"

"Well, I supposed to go home after cook Martha makes dinner. Cook leaves, too."

"So that leaves Esther alone in the house?"

"Yes, but not all nights. I having trouble with men at my house. It can be dangerous so sometimes I stay at Esther's house."

"Your house is dangerous, Ginny?"

"Yes. Some nights my boyfriend have friends. They play cards and drink. Then they want to do things with me. I have to run then."

"Ah, I understand. So Ester let you stay over on card night."

"Yes. She make a room for me up on third floor. No one knows but Esther."

Monica's eyes brightened. "Ah, I see. And were you in the house on the night of the murder?"

"Oh yes, I am there." (Expletives hurled out from the defendant's table.)

Judge, rapping gavel: "Silence! You've been warned."

"Tell us about that night, Ginny."

"After nine-thirty I hear Esther and some men shouting downstairs. There's screaming and running. Sounds like fighting. I am very scared."

"So you heard this from up in your room."

"Yes, and I take my cell phone. I should call 911, but I didn't because I afraid to speak. I crept down to second floor balcony and peep through the little bars of the rail."

"You could see them?"

"Yes, most of them. They are right below me. I see top half of Esther on floor by front door. She had rag in mouth and try to shout. One man put needle in her arm and other two holding her down. She struggle hard."

"Did you see anything more, Ginny?"

"I think they killing her. Maybe I next. I so scared. I go back to my room."

Ginny's head fell down in her hands.

"Take your time, Ginny. We understand. Did you see anything else?"

"I hear them go outside. I can see down on driveway. Two men carry Esther and drop her in black van. She not moving then. Someone else drive off in her car."

"That's all right Ginny. You did well. Anything else to add?"

"I should call 911." She shook her head and began to cry. "Wish I call 911 then but I think it too late. And maybe Izzy come back for me." Ginny looked at Esther. "I so sorry I not call police. So sorry."

"No, Ginny, we all understand. Did you leave then?"

"When everyone gone, I went to my home. Next day I came back and Martha said we are let go. They selling house. I leave town that day. I go to my cousins."

"Ginny, the other lawyer will ask you questions next. Are you up to it now, or should we ask for a recess?"

Ginny suddenly sat straight up. "Oh Ms. Monica, I am *ready*."

Monica grinned. "I think you are, too." She turned to the defense. "Your witness."

Wolfowitch's associate lawyer stood up and strode to the witness stand with determined precision. He paced back and forth before the stand with a contemplative expression. His first questions were aimed at the floor.

"So, Ms. Garcia, you are *very* good friends with Ms. Green?"

"Oh yes, but she Misses Brough back then."

"Uh huh, before the divorce. You would help Ms. Green in *any* way you could, wouldn't you"

"Oh yes. I would do anything for her."

He lunged toward Ginny and scowled close in toward her face. "*Anything*, huh? I'm sure you would. And I guess that would include telling one *sensational* make-believe story for her wouldn't it?"

Ginny looked puzzled. "You mean like read bedtime story?"

The attorney threw his head up and muttered something. "No, Virginia, I mean would you repeat an untrue story they told you to tell this court if she asked you?"

"Oh no Sir. Esther would *never* ask me to lie, and I swear to tell truth, yes?"

The lawyer moved in closer and raised his voice. "All right. Let's get down to it. You didn't *really* see who attacked your friend, Esther, that night, did you?"

"Not everyone. No. The man with needle, no. His back to me."

"And it was dark and you were a long way off, isn't that correct?"

She shook her head. "No, the lights were on and I was above them, maybe ten feet away. I see them good."

"But you haven't identified anyone, have you."

"Oh sorry. I only see side of Mr. Croft's face but it was him. I know his voice. And that man," she pointed at the defense table, "had Esther by the hair and her neck."

Sidney bolted up, eyes fixed on the pointing finger. "Why, you (expletive, "colorful" adjectives) *bitch*!"

Bailiffs came to restrain him when he tried to come around the table and the judge pounded his gavel for order. Izzy and W were having a heart felt conversation.

The attorney looked back at Ginny. "But the *final* truth is: you really have no proof of these accusations and this cleverly rehearsed story of yours, do you?"

Ginny's eyes widened. "Oh my goodness, I get so excited I forgot the pictures." She opened up her purse and took out her phone. "I took pictures with my cell phone. They still in here. Wait, I show you."

Wolfowitch shot up. "Your Honor, this is *new* evidence. We have had no time to examine it and it will require authentication. Defense requests a recess."

"Granted. Cell phone to FBI lab. Court is adjourned until tomorrow at nine o'clock."

Monica turned to Esther with an amazed expression. "You win, Esther. God is *real.*"

Esther chuckled. "*Always* real and always with us. We should talk about Him sometime."

Monica squeezed her shoulders and laughed.

WOLFTRAP

The trial collapsed rapidly around Izzy and Wolfowitch who mostly sat stone-faced while the lesser lawyers vainly tried to restore jury doubt about each witness. The FBI authenticated the photos on Ginny's cell phone as did the W's independent examiner. Monica presented the jury with dazzling enlargements showing Izzy's hand and his one of a kind ring still on his hand at the trial.

Izzy was lucky to get life in prison for the murder, but added to his sentence was a double attempted murder, assault and kidnapping. Forget parole. He would not escape prison in his lifetime.

When Esther was back on the stand she had pleaded for Izzy's life. "Give him a chance for salvation," she said. One woman in the jury wept loudly.

ROOTS

Myrna and Erik invited everyone to a casual poolside gathering to celebrate the trial's end. Jake showed up a half hour early and rapped on the guest house door for Esther.

"Hi, Jake. I like your party clothes."

He grinned. "Thanks. But if we can be serious for a minute, I'd like to talk with you in private. Is that all right?"

"Oh, sure." Esther gestured to the other side of the pool. "Let's sit over there in the shade."

They walked around balloon trees and waved at Erik who was changing the propane tank for his grill. Esther sat on a chaise chair and wrapped her arms around her knees. "What's up, Jake."

"Well, Esther, I had planned to surprise you by finding your mother for a wedding present. Unfortunately, I don't know where she is or even if she's alive. Couldn't find her."

Esther tilted her head. "That's all right. I never expected to ever see her, but thank you for your effort."

"Her trail went cold, but I did find out some things about her you might want to know."

"You're kidding. You know her name?"

"Only a maybe first name, Mary. But I had to look into your past too. I hope you don't mind."

She dropped her knees and leaned toward Jake in rapt attention. "No, not at all. Mary, huh?"

"Yes. You ran away from home when you were about thirteen. Mary ran away from home and parts unknown when she was sixteen."

"Really? How do you know that?"

"She turned up at the High Boots Bar in Vegas looking for a waitress job. The manager saw she was underage but gorgeous. He hired her as a stripper, and gave her a fake driver's license to cover their liability. The manager put her up in an efficiency room with another girl on their payroll."

"Wow. And you talked to these people?"

"Yeah, well, there's a different manager, but they keep files on employees in case they're challenged on the underage thing." He pulled out two pictures from his shirt pocket. "First one is their publicity shot, the other a copy of her illegal license."

Esther clapped her hand over her mouth and stared at the photos. Tears began to drip down her cheeks. "That's my *mom?*" she croaked.

"Age sixteen. Sorry about the almost no clothes one, but that's all they had."

"The license says Mimi McClain."

"Totally fictitious I assure you. It's her stage name. The address is for the room they gave her, but I tracked down her roommate from that."

"Could I talk to her?"

"Sure. I did. Her name is now Susi Brown. She lives in Redlands and is married with two children. Uh, I should caution you. Her husband has no knowledge about the stripper thing."

Esther laughed. "Well he *should,* but if I see her, I'll behave myself. What did she say about my mother?"

"Your mom was secretive and never said her last name. Mary might be made up too, but you'll like this. She wrote poetry."

"Awww, I got her writer's gene. But Susi has no idea where she is?"

"No. Mary had to quit work when she became pregnant but stayed at Susi's. A midwife delivered her right there. Three days later she was gone. As Susi recalls, her note read, 'Here's ten bucks for the cab. Your car is at the train station. Thanks for everything. Love, Mary.'"

"And that's it. No trace or clues?"

"Nada. She could be anywhere. Oh, but Susi did say she had a southern accent."

Esther pressed the photos to her chest. "Oh Jake, thanks for this. So much more than I hoped for. It's still a wonderful present. Now when I pray for her, I'll have her face in mind."

PARTY TIME

Jake and Price had transformed themselves into "different" people for Myrna's combination freedom and engagement party, wandering about in shorts and Hawaiian shirts. Even Monica swished in with her hair down, a cotton print dress and multicolored jogging shoes. Erik patted Bill on the shoulder. "Come on, we're the worker bees here. We've got hors d'oeurves to pass out and filets to grill."

Myrna swam ecstatically among the guests, filling drinks, and chatting. Off to one side, Esther and Ginny were laughing and talking, but Myrna interrupted them. "Esther Dear, the FBI has been looking into places for you to live when they close the safe house down. Well, guess what? We have the *perfect* place for you to stay until the wedding."

Esther touched her arm. "Myrna you've been so sweet and I've loved meeting you, but I'll get a job and rent a room somewhere."

"Not on your life. You and Bill are like family to us now." She pointed across the pool. "You're staying in our guest cottage where you were last night. Don't you even think of saying no."

Esther got up and gave her a hug. "But I'll pay you rent."

Myrna chuckled. "Family pays no rent, but you *can* help with the kids and some stuff around here, maybe tell my older boy about how real God is. He might listen to someone beside his mother."

Ester paused, not sure what to say, so Myrna bubbled: "Well, *that's* settled. I better get back to the kitchen before I burn the quiches."

Mountain scrunched his big head in between Esther and Ginny to announce that what was settled was petting time. Ginny scratched behind his ears, but suddenly her jaw dropped open. "Oh my gosh. I am so forgetful like my grandma already. This reminds me. I must tell you that little Barney is okay. I take him with me to my cousin."

Esther gave a joyful bounce and hugged her. "Ginny, that's *wonderful.* My little wiggly rescue boy? All these years I thought the worst."

"Yes, they shoot dogs. I know. I seen them. He come out of the closet when I called and I carry him out in sack. He *such* a good dog. How you ever teach him not to bark? It save his life."

"And he saved mine, Ginny. That little stray Jack Russell was all I had for company at night. How is he doing?"

"My cousin has two boys, six and nine. They play with him and spoil him lots. When you come and visit you can take him back."

"Oh, I'm so happy for Barney. No, the boys should keep him, but I would love to visit sometime soon, after the wedding for sure. He's no trouble is he?"

"No trouble, but they wonder why he no bark."

"Come on." She stood up. "Let's see what the others are up to, Ginny."

Erik's boys were coming out of the house wearing swim trunks but their dad stopped them. "Not now guys. This isn't a pool party. If you break that temporary screen around the pool, Mountain will get in for sure and you know what that means."

"Oh, Daaad."

"Seriously. You can go in later, but get some shirts on. We're about to eat anyway."

Myrna had the picnic table loaded with far more goodies than this casual gathering would entail but Jake was munching samples of everything there was. He also wandered through the party entertaining everyone with parlor tricks.

Bill and Esther were the first to sit. Linny appeared abruptly, gave Bill a quick wave "hi", but sat next to Esther. "Is it okay if I sit with you? I want to hear all about what it's like in prison."

Myrna was depositing a plate of mini quiches and overheard. She planted her hands on her hips. "Linny, now don't pester her too much, you hear?"

Esther tapped Liny on the shoulder. "I'd love to tell you everything, especially the part where Jesus came to visit."

Myrna concealed a delighted smile and turned back to the kitchen. Esther said, "I'll just give you a short version for now, but since I'll be living here for a few months we'll have lots of time to talk."

Pierce and Monica sat opposite them having a lively, laughing conversation about the trial, but by the time they finished the blueberry pie and Pierce had wiped off a blueberry smear on her cheek, she had accepted his invitation for a ride in his sailboat on San Diego Bay. Jake thumb pointed at them and pretended to whisper. "Looks like the sharks are swimming together."

Linny couldn't conceal her excitement. She leaned forward so she could look at Bill as well. "I'm so happy for both of you." She patted her chest. "This is so romantic. And, I have to tell you. I've already started on a wedding present for you. Two of them actually, but you can't peek 'til the reception."

Bill chuckled. "Could they be paintings, perhaps ?"

Linny swung her hair to one side and raised her nose faking a sophisticated air. "But of course, my dears." She giggled. "Oh but I finished 'Mountain Snowfall.' You can see that one if you want. I couldn't resist leaving in some of his impromptu additions."

The table bumped to one side as the big dog jockeyed for position near Linny's hand for the expected under table treats. She whispered, "Hang on guys. I think his plan is to turn over the whole table and jump in the food-fall."

Esther grinned at Linny, her eyes glistening. "I meant to ask you earlier. I'm hoping you will be one of my bridesmaids. Will you?"

Linny clapped her hands and chair-bounced. "Oh, yes. Love to. Thanks."

After the meal, Jake, Ginny and Monica said their goodbyes, but Pierce asked Erik if he could borrow a private room to chat with Bill and Esther. Erik nodded. "Sure. We better get out of the back yard anyway cause I'm about to let my boys clear away the pool fence. Besides, I should help Myrna with the dishes."

Bill and Esther snuggled close to each other on the burgundy leather loveseat in Erik's study. Bill whispered in her ear. "How does it feel to be *really* free, my love."

"I'm been free on the inside since I met Jesus." She rolled big eyes up toward him. "But free on the outside? It'll take some getting used to. I guess I've been in some sort of prison all my life, so you'll have to help me adjust."

Pierce pulled over a chair to face them, and produced his lawyer case. "Okay guys, just a few business items before I leave you two alone. Esther, you'll move out of the Safehouse tomorrow, but I want you to keep the emergency FBI call button Erik gave Bill, okay?"

"Yup. Already in my purse."

"Good." He reached into his brief case and took out a small picture frame surrounding a thick piece of glass with craters in it. "Here's a memento of your ordeal you can keep. Remember, we used this at the trial? It's a piece of the bulletproof glass we took from your car."

Bill held it up. "Wow, and a reminder of God saving our lives. Thanks, Pierce."

"You're welcome. And Esther, your car is out of impound and we replaced the glass. Hopefully you won't need the bulletproofing but we replaced it anyway. My treat."

Esther grinned. "Thanks. This is a treasure I want to show Rita when I visit her."

Pierce grinned and let out a big breath. "Okay, now for some *really* good news. Both of these came yesterday. The first is a check for you, Esther. It represents the first of three installments we got from the California settlement. The taxes and my fee are withheld, but your take-home is eighty four thousand. Nice wedding present, huh?"

Esther shook the envelope over her head. "Thank you Pierce, and the prison charities will thank you too."

He looked at Bill but pointed at Esther with a "can you believe this woman?' expression. "The final thing you'll like even more. I received a letter from Lucia's attorney. He *was* holding a letter she wrote for you. While her instructions were that he should only give it to you in person, I signed for it. Note that it has an intact seal."

Esther put her hands over her mouth and began tearing up so Bill took it and handed it to her. Pierce stood up. "The instructions also say that the attorney should *not* be present when you read it, so I'll be on my way." He picked up his bag.

"God bless you two. This has been one adventure none of us will soon forget."

Esther jumped up and gave him a parting hug. "May the Lord bless and keep you always, Pierce. Thank you *so* much for everything."

Bill gestured to Esther that he would leave her alone if she wished, but she told him to stay. She read the letter and cried, but when she reread it her forehead became furrowed. "Bill, how much cash do you have left?" Puzzled, he shook his head. "About a hundred ten thousand. Why, Dear?"

"We may have to buy Lucia's old house."

THE LETTER

Esther got up and went behind Erik's desk. "Bill, dear, would you go and tell our hosts we'll be in here a little longer? Also please ask Myrna if we might borrow a bible, and ask permission to use Erik's computer."

Bill scratched his head. "Esther, what the heck is in that letter?"

"I'll read it to you as soon as you get back." She grinned and waved him off. "Shoo."

Bill returned with an oversized leather bible. "Well, they gave me a funny look, but here it is." He plunked it down on the desk. "What's Lucia's note about?"

Esther handed him the letter and leaned back in the desk chair. "Maybe you should read it aloud, but slowly, okay?"

It was a single, handwritten page. "Here goes."

My Dearest Esther:

Although I have only known you a few months I feel like you are the granddaughter I never had. When you read this I expect to be with the saints above and you are no doubt wondering why I left you my house. It is because you are the closest thing I have to an earthly family, and I love you, my Dear.

Bill looked back at the envelope. "Was this written before the murder?"

"Yes, about a month before. She had no idea I'd be sent to prison. Keep going."

Now since you have the house, you should ask Uncle Matt for advice. Remember, you last saw him on the thirteenth and he talked about all the improvements he thought this house would need. Check what he wrote. He had forty four of them on his list.

Well, Dear, just rely on our ten step program, the one I kept drumming into you, and don't forget that important third step.

I am so proud of the growth you have had in the Lord, and I will rejoice to see you again one day in Heaven. Meanwhile, I pray the Lord will bless and keep you. May all your days be filled with love and joy.

Love,

Lucia Ross

Bill put the letter down and cocked his head. "Uncle Matt sounds even crazier than your so called grandmother. She wants you to go to AA and take the ten step program?"

Esther giggled. "Lucia was the brightest, most clear thinking person I ever knew, not to mention most loving. Neither of us drank, no wait, sometimes she would have a teeny sip of port after dinner. "

"Okay then, maybe she's not crazy, but that's one strange note."

"That's exactly what she wanted others to think. She wasn't sure someone else would see it, so it is written just for me."

"Because only you knew about the ten step program and Uncle Matt?"

"No. Only I would know there's *no such thing* as Uncle Matt and a ten step program. Also we studied the Bible a lot."

Bill gave her a crunchy-face stare until she giggled. "I think I can guess the passage, but open the Bible and read Matthew thirteen, verse forty-four."

Bill made an "O" with his lips as he searched for the passage. "It reads: The kingdom of Heaven is like a treasure hidden in a field. When a man found it he hid it again and then in his joy went and sold all he had and bought that field."

"Yup, that's the verse I thought it was."

"I think I get it." He thumped the Bible closed. "You think she might have something hidden on the property, something valuable."

"I do. She collected early antique photographs. Some of them are priceless, museum collectables."

"What about the ten steps that don't exist?"

"I'm not sure, but I'd guess she might mean ten steps from her back door to the fence. Perhaps the third pace is where she's buried something."

"Okay, so we should hope we can buy the house and go on a treasure hunt, huh? I guess we could always sell it again and hope to break even."

"You had better be the buyer, Bill. I don't want my name popping up in Las Vegas right now.

"No kidding. What's the address? I'll Google it right now."

Bill busied himself at the keyboard. "Okay, Esther, here it is. Bad news is it isn't on the market, but the good news, for us at least, is it went into foreclosure last week. I'll ask Jake to recommend a local realtor to keep an eye on it."

Esther went around the desk and gave Bill a hug and a smoochy kiss. "Good idea. He can let us know when it's on the market so you won't have to go running off to Vegas without me."

She turned on her pleading doe-eyes. "I really hope you'll stay near me particularly since I'm having that surgery next week."

"You know I will, darling."

"Myrna told me the receptionist at your work has a crush on you."

"Sweetheart, I've never given her more than a smile."

"Oh, good, cause two months from now I'd hate to marry a man in a wheelchair."

PRISONER FREEDOM

The Yard B walkers came to a stop when the PA system sounded the announcement buzzer, but some inmates dashed across the yard to get into position. "Attention everyone. There will be a concert from our Chapel Choir in the gymnasium at four o'clock today. Those normally using the gym at that time will be given Yard Passes if requested. The warden has authorized a thirty second preview for you, so hold down the noise, okay?"

Moneshia and three others stepped forward. A stick rapping on a canister beat out the rhythm taps: *ONE, TWO, THREE, FOUR...* The performers pointed their fingers up over the wall like an artillery salute and their voices were almost as loud. "One way, one way to Heaven—Hold up high your hands."

Opposite them in the Yard, four more stepped out, but with all hands raised and responded: “One way, free and forgiven, children of the Lamb.”

Moneshia stepped to the middle for her solo. “Two roads diverged in the middle of my life—I heard the wise man say.” (Chorus: badum, badum) “I took the one less traveled by and that’s made the difference, every night and every day.”

All eight moved to the center, raised their arms and sang: “So I say: one way, one way to Heaven, hold your heads up high. Follow, free and forgiven, Children of the sky.”

They bowed to applause and danced back into the crowd. The announcer said, “All right ladies, I know you won’t want to miss that this afternoon. See you there.”

Esther sat in a visitor’s booth patiently waiting. Finally, a large woman slid sideways past the entrance door from the inmate side. She bumped the guard getting through and was promptly scolded. Rita huffed into the chair facing Esther and pointed over her shoulder with her thumb. “That’s one narrow, little door. How’re you doing, Sweetheart?”

“I am just great, Rita. Anything interesting going on inside?”

"Changing every day, thanks to you. You should a heard the Chapel Concert we had this week. By the way you are the first visitor I've ever had in ten years in this clink. Nice to see you. Oops, I lied. My gang sent me their hot shot lawyer nine years ago. He said he'd have me out in a month."

"So you had a trial review?"

Rita looked up at the ceiling and shook her jowly cheeks. "Nah, never heard from him again. So what brings you back here? Say, if you miss the place, maybe we could arrange a swap."

Esther chuckled. "I just wanted to see you. First, I'm sorry I couldn't arrange for you to be in my wedding."

"Well, I don't…" She released a low laugh that heaved her large frame. "I wouldn't make a real attractive bridesmaid, hon. But say, I'm real glad you got free—all of us are. And you did get Nancy to be in it. She'll tell us all about it."

"Oh, she will, and probably things I wouldn't want anyone to hear." She reached into her bag and brought out the glass in a frame. "Know what this is?"

Rita reached in her pocket and slipped on a pair of glasses. She squinted and moved in as close as she could. "Sure, bullet holes. Looks like a forty-five at close range, but no penetration. Test panel for protective glass, right?"

"No, Rita, this is you saving my life—Bill's too. Izzy tried to keep me from testifying, or even *living,* but we were in the car you gave me."

She slapped the counter with a big grin. "No (expletive)! Oops, pardon my French. That's so *great.* Izzy's lower than a worm. He really got what he deserved."

"Bill and I can't thank you enough. We wouldn't be having this conversation if you hadn't given me that car."

Still grinning, she shook her head. "That's the third piece of glass I had to replace on the driver's side. All cars oughta have the stuff like standard issue, don't you think?" Her expression became pensive. "But here's a weird thing. You know how when your born again Spirit-Person starts changing you on the inside, uh, kinda poking you around to do things?"

"Oh, yes."

"Yeah, you called 'em 'nudges,' I think. Well, when you were released I got a big time nudge to give you that army tank of a car. No credit here. It's a God thing."

"Praise the Lord. How are you doing with Him?"

"Oh, ha-ha, I'm on some kind of a trip with the Big Guy, Ms. Greenie. Can you believe I'm listening to other people's problems and really caring? They let us start help groups for some what really need it. The really weird thing is I think I'm the one they help most. I've never felt better about what I'm doing. It's a trip all right. Say, you tearing up?"

Esther nodded. "I am. You can't know how happy it makes me to see this change in you. You're doing a mighty work for Christ, and you look just beautiful."

"Beautiful, huh? But you know what, Esther? I've got some *real* friends now. People who care about how I'm doing, like you do, and I love 'em. But here's something amazing I discovered. It's about the 'forgive others' and love your enemies' thing. God told me to forgive this creep, someone I've hated for years. I mean a *real* creep—know what I mean?"

"Were you able to?"

"Not at first, but I said to God, I said 'you gotta help me with this'. Well he sure did. He actually washed away my anger so much, I had to write her. And she was really impressed, too. She's gonna visit me next month—and she even sounds like a real person now. "

"An amazing God we have, Rita. Any others coming to know Him in Yard B?"

"Oh yeah, but here's a tip. It's fine that people from the outside come in and bring some to Christ, but these inmates need friends on the inside. They really need people who care to look after them every day, like Nancy does for me. Then what happens is we do our own God support thing. We have a group that crochets blankets. Every new believer gets one. Another group makes 'God Loves You' wall signs for all the new inmates. Our Chaplain lady can hardly believe us."

"Oh, she's such a cool woman. How about when she sang a duet with Moneshia?"

"Yeah, this God thing is so all over Yard B, we're starting missionary work."

Esther laughed. "*Missionary* work? They're not letting you out are they?"

"Sort of. We got delegations to go over to Yard A. They're supposed to be the tough guys, but Paul said it's God's will that none should perish, didn't he? So we gonna go convert 'em all. You'll see."

The buzzer sounded. Esther shook her head and grinned. "God bless you, Rita. I came here to try and boost *your* spirits, but now I'm the one on a high.

BACKYARD BUZZ

One month later Bill and Esther were knocking on the door of the Simms house. Myrna flung it open. "Oh, my goodness! What have you done to my precious Esther?" She put her face in close and gingerly touched the purple bloating around her right eye. "Beaten in prison, and now beaten outside, huh?"

Esther put her arms around Myrna and squeezed. "Oh, this man's terrible. Beats me cause I just don't *listen*, but now I'll be a better wife. You'll see."

Chuckling, Myrna held her at arms length. "You're a sassy one, aren't you? But seriously, does it hurt?"

"Not really—a little tender to touch is all. Bandages came off yesterday."

Bill said "Oh she's fine, all right. Esther's already convinced her plastic surgeon to reconcile with his wife and begin pastoral counseling."

Myrna laughed heartily and hugged her. "Come on in you troublemaker, and have a seat in Erik's Lazy Boy. Care for some lemonade?"

Bill said, "Yeah, great. We're parched."

Myrna's eyebrows raised. "And was I talking to you?"

Esther chuckled. "Yes, please. We'd love some."

Bill escorted her to the recliner. "Myrna sure likes you, doesn't she?"

Esther eased back partway and nodded. "Yeah, and now I know what it's like to have a real mother. I have to admit, it feels pretty good."

"Yup, she's a tour-de-force mother all right, but we're both going to spoil you post-surgery, so get used to it."

"Mother" bustled back in with three lemonades on a tray and a bowl of cookies. "I heard you two arguing a few weeks back about this operation. Notice my restraint in not asking why."

She passed the drinks out and pulled over a chair. "Okay, restraint's over. Tell me why this beast dragged you off to a surgeon. And I used to like him, too."

Esther was getting the giggles, but she took a long sip through the curved straw. "Well, at first I thought this-- this *beast…*" She laughed, put her glass in the armrest cup holder, and looked up at Bill. “This beast, just wanted me to look prettier.”

“Sounds just like a man. Turn you right back into a trophy wife, huh?”

Esther laughed. “No, he…” She reached for a cookie. “Oh you explain, Bill. This is delicious, by the way, Myrna.”

Bill pouted at Myrna. “Not that it’s any of your business--but here’s the thing. plastic surgeons do reconstructive type surgery too. From one or more face smashes our fairy princess had a broken nasal septum and zygoma too.”

“A zigo, what?”

“Zygomatic bone, part of the cheek bone, an arch of bone below the eye. Hers was fractured and separated. Not only did it cause a flatter face look, but key facial nerves go through a hole in this bone. Another bump and she could’ve had facial paralysis.”

“Oh.” Myrna patted her arm. “You poor dear.”

“So, the surgeon reconstructed the arch and her nose as well. She could only breathe on one side you know. Of course my Este kept arguing she could live with all that.”

Myrna scowled at Esther. “And I hope you weren’t thinking it was God’s will for you to suffer.”

"Maybe a little, but see, I'm not used to being with people who actually love me."

Myrna got up and kissed Esther on the forehead. "Well you *better* get used to it, little one. And speaking of your loving fans, Ginny was going to be here to surprise you when you came but she got held up in traffic."

"Really?" Esther sat up. "I better take my things to my room and change."

Myrna helped her stand. "My boys already carried your bags to the guest house. Linny will help you get settled." She scowled at Bill. "And you better not go in there."

He laughed. "Gosh, just when I thought I'd been redeemed."

Later, Linny and Esther emerged from the guest house, Mountain wagging a great tail behind them. Linny bounced over to her mom and gestured toward Esther. "There, doesn't she look better? She let me put on some makeup over the purple stuff."

Esther reached down to rub Mountain's cheek. "And now my face is her latest watercolor." She gestured toward the orange traffic cones placed around the edge of the lawn. "So what's all this?"

Myrna's look was sheepish. "I, well you were in the *hospital* and no one has done any real wedding plans. I, er, just thought I'd lay something out in case you might like it. You can change anything you don't like, of course."

"Sure. Whatcha got?"

Myrna's face became ebullient as she pranced over to a line of cones. "So here's where the head table will be, not far from the guest house so you can change or whatever. And over here will be the drink bar."

She skipped along the edge of the pool. "And down about here is where the band will set up, so you can use this paved area to dance. The caterer will set up the buffet on the patio, and of course all this furniture will be gone."

Laughing and head shaking, Esther gave Myrna a hug. "But 'mother', there's not going to be that many people. Neither Bill nor I have any relatives."

Myrna put her hands on her hips. "And of course that explains why I had to send out the invitations for you."

Esther thrust her head forward, open mouthed. Bill said, "Oh no. Who the heck did you invite?"

With an impish grin, Myrna waved them over to the patio. "Come on, let's chat about that." She gestured for them to sit.

Esther plunked herself down but kept her gaze fixed on her. She lowered her eyebrows. "Myrna?"

She twirled her hand around as she eased into a chair. "Oh, there'll be a few guests. First, I invited everyone from Bill's little church where you'll have the service, of course. I had a little chat with Reverend Tim. He's so nice. He estimated that fifteen or twenty would attend and come to our reception, and then there's Tim's family as well.

"Tim suggested a rehearsal for the wedding party. We scheduled that the day before, and I thought we'd have the rehearsal dinner here, but Pierce *insists* on us being his guests. Monica knows the perfect restaurant, he says. Let's trust them on that. Those two have been hanging out together since the trial, and I notice she leads him around on a string."

Bill took Esther's hand but shook his head at Myrna. "But wait a minute. Wedding party?"

"Of course. Just a small one, but there's three groomsmen and three bridesmaids, and, of course, the pastor and his wife plus us. Erik will walk you down the aisle unless you have someone else in mind."

Esther said, "Myrna! I never asked you to do all this. I thought we'd just have a simple reception after. There's an Olive Garden near the church."

Myrna laughed. "My Dear, I guess I should confess: I *live* for this kind of thing. But just wait and see how much fun it'll be."

"Okay, who else did you invite. I only know about Nancy from prison."

"Ngami Bhutto? Yes, and she'd make a perfect Maid of Honor except she'll only get two days out of prison. Linny will be a bridesmaid, but you might want to consider Ginny for the head position. 'Course there's Maria Diaz, too. Think about it."

"The prison guard?"

"Yes, and she's so delighted to be invited. She'll come with her husband and another couple who are friends of theirs."

"I should be very angry with you, Myrna. You've been doing all this without asking. Truth is, I'm deeply touched, but come clean. Who else did you invite?"

Myrna giggled. "Sure, well there's about eight people from our office that Bill knows, and of course Mary Stearns and Judy Pyle."

Bill said, "Oh yeah, those two *should* come. They saved our lives you know."

"Yes, and they're coming with two of the guys from Judy's motorcycle gang. Do you know what the gang's called?"

Bill shook his head. "I think we were a little too busy to notice at the time."

"Their gang's called, 'Ride On King Jesus'. Don't you just love it?"

Ester bounced on her chair. "Oh, oh, that's right. I saw one of them go by before we went into the park."

"Finding Mary was easy. She's performing stand up comedy downtown, and what a character she is, too. Mary has about a hundred words for every one of Judy's. Hard to believe these two are friends."

Bill nodded. "Judy's a writer, not a talker, but prison friends have a forever bond like soldiers. Isn't that right, darling?"

"Sure do, and I'm so glad they're coming. Is that it, Myrna?"

"Pretty much. There's a few of our friends too." She raised an eyebrow at Bill. "It's up to you to invite your brother from Connecticut."

"Half brother—haven't heard from him for many years." He patted Esther's arm. "Myrna has access to my complete data file as you can tell."

Esther took hold of his hand. "You hadn't mentioned him, but Bill, he's family nonetheless. Don't you think it's best to reconcile any differences?"

Bill nodded.

Myrna straightened up and grinned. "Well good. That's all settled. All right my dear, do you want to shop for a wedding dress?"

"I suppose so, but I'll get a rental, I think."

Myrna looked around to see if anyone was listening. She whispered, "You mustn't tell anyone, but I have a new dress in my closet and I think it's your size."

Esther leaned in and whispered back. "Cool. Was it the one you wore?"

"No, it's new. I know it sounds crazy, but I bought it last year for Linny."

"What? You bought a wedding dress for your teen age daughter?"

"Shhh, shhh. It's just so beautiful and it was on sale. I think it will be her size when she grows up and gets married."

"*If* she gets married."

"I know, I know, but I'm a little nutty about the marriage thing, can't you tell?"

Grinning nods from Esther and Bill who said together: "We can tell."

"Anyway dear, you should try it on. No pressure to wear it, but you won't find anything with the simple beauty this one has." Her cell phone rang. "Hold on a sec.

"Uh huh. You are real close, then. The GPS sometimes messes up. Just go south on the boulevard you're on and turn left on Pine Street. Second left and look for ten twenty on your right." She hung up her phone. "Ginny's almost here."

When the bell rang, Esther bounded over to greet her friend. Ginny stood beside a tall man in a business suit. His chiseled handsome face sported a dark mustache. "Esther, this is my husband, Ernesto."

She hugged them both. "Wow, I can't tell you how glad I am to see you two. Come on in."

Ernesto spoke in perfect English. "The pleasure is all mine."

After the introductions they all gathered back on the patio. Ginny patted her husband's shoulder. "Ernesto owns a roofing business, and he encouraged me to take English lessons. How's this? For several months I have been studying the American spoken language at our nearby institution."

Esther laughed. "Ginny, that's wonderful. I think you even used a past perfect presence or something in there."

Ginny grinned. "That is not what my instructor calls it, my dahling."

All laughed. Ginny reached into her purse and pulled out some photos. "I could have e-mailed these to you, but I want to give them to you in person." She handed them to Esther. "They are all Barney pictures. See how he play with my nephews? They teach him tricks, too."

Esther chuckled at the photos and passed them on. "I'm so happy he's in a good home and I promise to visit one day soon when we come up and see you. But, Ginny, are you as nervous as I am? You're okay about being in this wedding?"

"Oh yes. I'm excited, but I am not sure of all I must do."

"Not to worry, Ginny. Myrna here has *everything* under control."

SAN DIEGO NEWS HERALD

JUNE 12, 2012, Section C8:

Local Marriages

William Harrison Mason from Hartford, Connecticut and Esther Green of Las Vegas were married at The Christian Fellowship Church in El Cajon on Saturday. A reception was held in the home of Erik and Myrna Simms following the service.

HONEYMOON

Esther and Bill relaxed, side by side on a lounge chair. The balcony in their honeymoon suite overlooked sailboats enjoying the breeze in San Diego Bay. She wiggled a bit against him. "Don't let it go to your head, but you're one handsome dude in a tux."

"Thank you. And you really look much better now that your nose in the center of your face."

"Esther suppressed a giggle. "And I'm amazed at how you know the perfect nuanced words to compliment a woman."

"Thank you."

"Amazed."

Bill turned his head toward her a bit and rubbed her shoulder. "But, Kitty Cat, I might also point out that you are one passionate, sexy monster."

She snickered and kissed the shoulder-rubbing hand. "But only for *you*, my sweetum hunk."

Bill sighed. "It was nice I got that teaching job starting in the fall. Unfortunately for you, Mrs. Mason, I now realize you're going to keep me too tired to work."

Esther's large eyes became beacons of innocence. "Perhaps we should get separate bedrooms?"

He snatched a hand and pretended to munch on her fingers. "Ah, too late. My addiction is terminal."

She gave him a little slap and relaxed back in her lounge chair. "This has truly been the best few days of my life, Bill. Nothing in the earthly realm could top this."

Esther giggled. "But could anyone have predicted that Mountain would slip through the pool barrier at just the right moment and terrorize our wedding guests?"

"But you," he shook his head, "*you* had your back turned and threw the bouquet anyway, just as he released the shower."

"Ha, ha. I heard screaming but I figured they were jostling for position."

"Everyone scattered except for Linny. She slid in, grabbed the dog's collar with one hand and caught the flowers with the other. I hope Erik's video shows it. She looked like a second baseman stretching for an out."

"Yup, she nabbed the bouquet all right, and maybe she really will use that dress in a few years. She's such a talented girl. And can you believe the gorgeous watercolors she painted for us? You should put the one with the planet thing in your classroom."

"That's Saturn with its moons, and I wonder what she did to make the rings shimmer like they do. But the one of us with the angels is big time gallery quality."

Esther threw her head back and looked up. "Oooh. There we are, all dressed for the wedding and starting down a long windy road, but overhead she painted two stunning angels watching over us. There couldn't be a more beautiful wedding present. I just love it."

"It's a real treasure, and so was our 'not so little' wedding. Tell me, what did you imagine our wedding would be like before Myrna did her magic?"

Esther sighed and took a sip of sparkling lemon water. "I pictured myself wearing an evening gown and a little pill box hat with a veil, maybe a dozen guests, tops."

"Kinda what I thought. I was ready to reserve the Olive Garden across the street for our guests. I'm not into fancy stuff, but I have to say, that was really fun. Myrna really knows how to put on a wedding."

"Ya think?"

Bill chuckled. "But it's too bad Nancy had to go back to prison. She's served six of her ten years. Pierce said that her crime had sentencing guidelines of only three to six years. I'm going to ask him to put in for a sentence review."

"Bill, Pierce told me it could be protested formally, but that could be expensive."

"Maybe we could help her later, Esther, but right now we'll have to put all our cash into that house in Vegas. It's just about to go on the market, and the realtor Jake found for us says she's right on it. She promises to let us know what to bid this week."

Esther got up, leaned on the rail and inhaled the sea air. "Back to real life again tomorrow, huh?"

"Yup, no more sailing, swimming and massaging. Oh, I meant to talk to her, but what's Mary Stearns up to these days? I'm glad Linny and Ginny convinced her to give a maid of honor speech. I'm still laughing."

Esther chuckled. "Oh, that woman is something else. She told me she got a job as a comedienne driver-guide on San Diego's Trolley Tour, and she does stand up comedy on weekends. I wanted her to catch my bouquet."

"What I don't understand is how a woman like her gets to be friends with a Judy Pyle."

"That's interesting, isn't it? Maybe opposites attract, but Judy approached her and invited her to learn how to ride a cycle. Also, Mary's the only one who can make her laugh. And get this: in an after-ride party, some of the gang witnessed their faith to her and they talked for hours. In the end Mary accepted Christ into her heart."

"You guys don't mess around, do you?"

Esther chuckled. "Nope. And as only Mary could put it, 'One minute I could care less, then slam, bang, wow, God is real.' They voted her into the Ride On King Jesus gang, and that was just days before they saved us in the park."

Bill stood next to his balcony-gazing wife and slipped his arm around her waist. "That's so cool. All right my love, tomorrow we do have to face real life again and face the first crisis in our marriage."

"So tell me, Prince Charming, what might *that* be?"

"Well, not only are you going to have to go back and risk being shot in Las Vegas, but I…"

"Wait, let me guess. You have another wife in Iran. No, you have a million dollar gambling debt and the mob just found you?--Something else?"

"Yes, and it's worse, much worse."

Esther's jaw dropped. "What?"

"I never cleaned out my bachelor apartment."

HOUSE HUNTING

"This street looks almost deserted, Esther. Sure it's the right one?"

"Absolutely. We just passed Jimmy's old place. I ought to know it, right? See, there's still a 'For Sale' sign outside. Just pull into the driveway."

"Heck, we just spent all our cash on *this*? Look at the lawn: dead grass a foot high and paint peeling off everywhere. Obviously the internet photos were from the first sale."

Ester got out the passenger door and leaned back in to look at Bill. "Now, dear, what did you expect? It's been in foreclosure a long time." She chuckled. "Besides, it looks neat compared to your apartment."

"Very funny."

Bill had just closed his door and was right behind Esther when she froze, turned around and whispered. "Bill, the kids from the gangster across the street are on the porch."

They were slinking back to their car, but a hail from the porch stopped them again. "Hey, is that you, Esther?"

She planted a smile on her face before turning as casually as possible. "Oh, hi Johnny. I see Sammy right behind you. How are you guys?"

Sammy, the younger at age ten, came up and hugged Esther. "We missed you and granny Lucia. Dad said you were in penitentiary but he didn't know what happened to granny."

Esther thought, *Oh yes he did,* but said, "I got out when they found I was innocent. Poor granny passed away."

"Darn." They said together.

Esther put her hand on Bill's shoulder. "I'm married now and this is Bill, my husband."

Bill gave them fist bumps. "Nice to meet you guys."

Esther said, "Would you two do me a favor and not mention I was here to your father? Can you do that?"

Johnny pointed his finger like a revolver. "No sweat. Dad's divorced and in Federal prison in Arizona."

Esther was embarrassed by her spontaneous grin. "Oh, sorry to hear that. Hope your mother is doing okay."

"Yeah, she's back in school," He rolled up his eyes. "And she got all 'churchy'. Makes us go every week."

Esther giggled. "Well, that can't be too bad. Jesus can be like a father to you if you let Him."

Sammy kicked at some dirt. "Yeah, that's what mommy said too, but I'm hoping for her new boyfriend."

Johnny tapped his brother on the shoulder. "Come on we gotta get back for lunch. You buy this place?"

"Yes, but we bought it for a rental. We won't live here, but we'll come and go, so we'll see you again." They waved and headed out across the street with their skateboards. "Good to see you boys. Come over anytime. God bless."

Bill looked at Esther and crossed his eyes. "Well, that could have been worse."

Esther said, "I'll say. No telling what the syndicate might do if they cornered me."

"Probably nothing, but I understand."

She used the code on the realtor lock, took the keys and went in. The empty house was startling. The angry, foreclosed-upon owners left a wreck which was now decorated with cobwebs. There were gouges and holes in the wallboard, and the carpet was half torn off in the living room.

Esther and Bill peeked into the kitchen. Bill shrugged. "They even took the stove and microwave."

“But look,” Esther said, her voice like a morning bird. “They left the kitchen sink.”

Bill chuckled. “Probably because their pickup was full up.” He turned to the side door. “Oh, what’s that, a mouse?”

“Very funny.”

He bent down and picked up something wedging the screen door open. “Hmm, piece of mahogany—probably broken off the furniture.” He tossed it to his wife.

Esther gasped and put it against her cheek.

“Darling, what is it?”

“It’s the scroll.” She turned it over in her hands. “Lucia’s—it’s been broken right off.”

Bill rubbed his ear. “I don’t get it—scroll?”

“The top of Lucia’s violin. The mobsters must have thrown it against the wall when they took over. I’ll bet it was that mean guy across the street, too.” She sighed and slipped it into her satchel purse.

Bill came close and put his arms on her shoulders. “Sorry, dear. Not a very nice souvenir.”

“Guess not, but I’m glad to have it anyway. I’ll remember her music every time I see it.” Esther went to the slider leading into the back yard and slid it open. The back lawn looked like the front: dead. “Bill, I sat on lawn chairs right under that tree, and that's where I came to accept Jesus as Lord."

"And it's here where we are supposed to dig, huh? I'll get my tools."

Esther went back to the slider when he returned and counted the paces to the back fence. "Bill, I think it's about ten steps all right, but I can't walk into the dead roses."

"Okay, but three paces puts it right here at the edge of the concrete patio." Bill tried to get his shovel into the ground. "Man it's just hard pan here. Don't think it's been dug into for many years at least. Maybe she meant three paces from the side fence gate. That would end up in the shrubs, at least."

Esther hunted for any sign of digging while Bill proceeded to put holes in the old boarder garden and scratch his arms on the roses. Finally, he dropped his shovel. "Well dear, guess what? We could get a backhoe and shave the whole yard, but I honestly don't think your little old lady buried anything back here."

"Sorry. Lets take a break inside and get out of the sun. I'll get some water from the cooler."

The two settled down on a relatively clean place near the front door and leaned against the wall. She took out a cold bottle from her satchel for him, and patted at his forehead with a Kleenex. "Just rest awhile, dear, and don't be discouraged. Remember our plan. We still can fix the place up and sell it."

Bill sipped the water in silent thought for awhile. "What's up those stairs, darling?"

She shrugged. "Oh, just two of the tiniest guest rooms you ever saw, but there's a bath room between them."

He sighed. Suddenly, he grabbed her arm. "Esther!"

"Ouch, you startled me."

"Esther, there are *ten* steps in that staircase."

They jumped up and ran to inspect them. The stairs were covered with green shag carpet, filthy and worn but still intact. "Don't forget the important third step, she said."

Bill walked up to the third step and tramped on it with his foot. It made a little 'clunk' sound. He looked back down at Esther and grinned. "Third step is a little loose, my dear."

He wiggled the step, but it seemed firm. Bill felt along the carpet below the lip of the stair. On each end it pulled away revealing a slide lock going up into the stair plate above. Esther knelt on the first step admiring his discovery. "Do you really think it's hollow under there?"

"Oh yeah." He released both slides and pulled. The stair was carefully grooved and slid outward with ease. "Ta taaa!"

Esther jumped up and peered in. "Photographs! Old sepia ones." She eagerly slid the top layer into her hand and went toward the back slider for more light to examine them. "Oh, these are *wonderful*, Dear. Here's one of Wilson's inauguration, and another of the Eiffel tower being built." Bill, we can't sell these. They're too precious.

Back on the stairs, Bill was making banging noises. "And look. Here's one in the old wild west and…"

Bill came over and sat next to her, but he looked into her eyes, not the photos. "What, Bill? You're looking funny. Don't you want to see these?"

He held up a plastic cylinder for her to see. "Know what this is?"

She squinted at the object. "A stack of coins. I think she collected half dollars too. She liked the ones with real silver in them. But look at *this* photo I think it's actually Henry Ford's first car coming off the line."

"They're gold coins, dear."

Esther looked up at him. "Oh, are they old ones? Maybe a collector would buy them."

"Nah, they're only twenty, thirty years old, tops."

"Oooh, but look at this picture. I think it's the first cast at a new opera house in Los Angeles and someone *signed* it on the back."

Esther studied Bill's face. "Why are you still looking so funny? Look, if there's gold in the coins they must be worth something. Why don't you see if anybody is interested in buying them? You're good on the Internet."

Bill laughed. "Esther these are one ounce gold bullion coins. Each one is worth about fifteen hundred dollars."

She patted his arm. "Oh, that's *great.* Maybe we'll have enough to fix this house up for resale after all. Are there enough?"

"Oh yes. But Esther…"

"Well, it's settled then. I'm going to get a display album for these photos. A museum curator should see them. Look at this one. I'll bet it's the Scopes trial in Tennessee."

Bill could hardly talk. The giggles had overtaken him. He grasped her cheeks with both hands and turned her face to his. "Stop talking a moment, o precious one. Each cylinder contains twenty coins. There are three hundred and ten of these cylinders. Darling, we own over nine million dollars worth of gold."

Slowly an "O" formed on her lips. "I guess God wants us to start up a foundation."

Bill couldn't contain his laughter. "Darlin-oh *sweetie!* You have no idea how beautifully unique you are, do you?" He held her face again, now covered with innocent puzzlement and gave her forehead a kiss. "The first, maybe the first *million* wives, would have exclaimed, 'wow, honey, we're rich', but you…" He had to laugh again. "But you, *you* say let's start a foundation."

She put her hand on his cheek. "It will be to help prisoners find the Lord, darling. You're not annoyed with me, are you?"

Bill kissed her gently on the lips. "Esther, you are just *the* most wonderful woman in the world and you don't even know it. Thank you for loving an old scoundrel like me. I admit, I was toying with the suggestion of you keep the photos and I keep the coins, but even though we're married, I know this is all *your* money. You should spend it anyway you wish."

"Well, we wouldn't have to use *every* bit to start up the foundation. We could afford to pay Pierce to help Nancy, and--and you should take ten percent, at *least* ten percent, and spend it on anything you want."

"Far more than I deserve, my dearest. I can live with ten percent."

PART THREE

LOS ANGELES, CA.

TEN YEARS LATER

CMN NEWS

Whoever acknowledges me before men,

I will also acknowledge him before my

Father in Heaven Mt 10: 32

"Mrs. Mason, are you comfortable sitting here? It will help me if you can be still. I really need to get you ready before you go on."

Esther smiled at the young woman who confronted her with an anxious expression. "Excuse me, what's your name?"

She swung her long brown tresses to one side. "Oh sorry, I'm Kayla."

"Call me Esther. Kayla, couldn't we just we skip the makeup? I'm not used to wearing any."

Kayla planted her makeup box on a nearby table and sat on a stool in front of Esther. She pleaded. "I'm real sorry, Esther, but if you go in there with any hot spots showing, I could lose my job."

"Okay, maybe just touch *those* spots, but I really don't like stuff on my face."

"Esther, I just want to say I have so much respect for you. I read that what you like to do most in the whole world is bring people to Jesus, and that's wonderful. But what I like most is to make a perfect face for the camera. These freckles of yours will look like raisin bran under the lights with Hi-Def. You sure you don't want a little touch up?"

Esther made a face.

Kayla brushed powder on her forehead. "You've got a thin scar under this eye, and ooh, there's a big one on your forehead."

She squinted, moved closer to Esther's eye, and pouted. "Now don't you let that Miss Pris push you around. You just hold you're ground. I'll be out here rooting for you."

Esther held up her hand to gently ward her off. "No more makeup today, all right?" But tell me: how do you feel about Jesus?"

"I guess I'm okay' with Him, but say, I've an idea. How about if you let me do my job now, then afterward you can pray with me or whatever you want. How's that sound?"

Esther laughed. "Deal. Slap it on, sister."

A man with dark curly hair and headphones bustled over, bent down and squinted into Esther's eyes. Black things attached to his belt and wires flailed about whenever he turned. He pointed with a clipboard. “All right Ma’am, you’ll be on in just a minute. Watch your introduction on this monitor. If Pricilla says anything wrong about you, you’ll want to correct it. Are you nervous?”

Esther was staring at his black T shirt that said “I see dead pixels.” “Of course I’m nervous, sir. This is live national TV, right?”

He clipped a mini mike to her lapel. “International.”

Kayla slid her box to one side. “There.” She lightly put her hand on Esther’s arm. “Don’t you worry, Esther. Just pretend you’re in a living room alone with that Miss Prissy, and don’t let her nastiness bother you one bit. Good luck.” She smiled and gave her arm a squeeze.

“Thanks, Kayla.”

The monitor blinked on and a large boned blonde woman with big hair smiled at the camera. “Welcome back to ‘Pris’s Corner’ everyone. Our next guest is a remarkable young woman. Ten years ago she was in prison for murder and today she is the CEO of the billion-dollar Lucia G Ross Foundation. She heads up their program called ‘Prisoner Freedom’, a program credited for the early release of many prison inmates. Recent studies have shown their efforts have reduced repeat offenders, and their donations increase every year.

"Her biography, "Este-Este," is on the best sellers list right now, and she also writes children's books, yet she lives in a modest home in suburban San Diego with her husband and two children. Let's find out what's behind this powerhouse of the charitable world. Please give a warm Pris's Corner welcome to Esther Green Mason."

Esther ambled across the set to the applause of the studio audience. She grinned at the people, gave them a little 'Hi' wave, shook hands with Priscilla and sat on the maroon leather couch.

Priscilla began, "We don't usually entertain charities at Pris's Corner, but our producers insisted on an exception in your case considering the explosive growth in your foundation. Let's find out why. Esther, are your contributions coming in from relatives hoping to get early releases for prisoners in their families?"

Esther shrugged. "Personally I think the reason is our obedience to the Lord's work. Others say it's the transformational effect on inmates before and after their release. But it is true we assisted in the early release of eighty-two so far this year."

"Well that's significant. And we certainly hope that at least some of those people were *innocent*." She paused, hoping for studio laughter. "Is that why your organization is called Prisoner *Freedom?*"

"No, it's for another reason, Priscilla. Is this show live or recorded?"

"We're on live, baby, unless you say some *really* bad words, then we'll bleep you with our ten second delay."

Esther's smile was demure. "I'll try to avoid those. We've actually helped free thousands of prisoners who still remain behind bars. We've helped them to a more important freedom: freedom from their past sins by their acceptance of salvation through Jesus Christ. Their daily work is now for the Kingdom and they have a newfound joy."

"That sounds so sweet, but they're still locked up, aren't they? Tell us what your group actually *does.*"

"If you haven't found the Lord, His love and His purpose for your life, Priscilla, our work may seem foolish to you."

"I think you're telling us you just make inmates happier. Wouldn't you get the same result if you just slipped them some pot?" Priscilla relished the audience tittering.

"Having found the reality and love of Christ, those people who are still locked up in prison are happier and more secure than you are."

A brief flash of anger crossed Priscilla's face, but quickly passed. She tried to brush her hair aside, but the whole hair set swiveled to one side and back. "So, Esther, how does it feel to be an important person now, telling everyone what's right and what's wrong?"

"Important?" She dropped her head a little and smiled. "Any 'importance' in this world is just a stumbling block. I'm awed that God would choose someone like me for His Holy work. The Lord has a place and a mission for everyone if they only reach out and accept it. My greatest joy comes each time I see a happy peace come over a new face."

"Well, I'm told you were going to bring one of those *happy* people with you. We're sorry that didn't work out."

"I tried to negotiate a temporary release for my friend, Rita Clough. She used to be 'Big Rita' in the Los Angeles syndicate and her time is up in a year. Unfortunately, our state still seems unable to trust her on the outside."

Priscilla turned to the audience and feigned a puzzled expression. "And I wonder why that could be."

"Rita was so excited about finding God a decade ago, she became a true inspiration to me and others. She's done some absolutely *wonderful* things inside the prison, particularly with the addicts."

"All right, let's move on. Our promise to Pris's Corner guests is to give them time to plug their books. Tell our viewers about the most important book they should read."

"That would be The Holy Bible, Priscilla." Audience laughter.

Pris's lower lip crashed into the upper. "I mean your books, of course, Ms Mason. You get to plug *your* books."

"My biography, "Este-Este?" It was written by a ghost writer, and kind of boring so I'd skip that one." The audience laughed. "My children's books are written for the four to seven year olds. They are bedtime stories with biblical principals. It's so important for parents to spend one on one time with their children, and bedtime is very special."

"What about you husbands book?"

"Oh, yes. Bill wrote a book called "Coincidence or God?" It's about the amazing things God does in this world. Sold really well in its first year 'cause he's such a good writer. He teaches writing courses too. Want to hear more about it?"

"Sorry, we have to go to commercial break, but when we come back lets hope we can peek behind the scene and find out what's *really* going on at Prisoner Freedom."

During the break, Priscilla's face lost her on-camera smile. She leaned in to talk privately. "Mrs. Mason, you agreed to our terms in coming here. No proselytizing. That means no witnessing about Jesus, you hear? This ain't the 700 Club, lady. Understand?"

Esther shrugged.

The man with flailing wires stepped onto the set. "Ten seconds, Pris."

Priscilla's face resumed its radiance as the camera light came on. "Welcome back everyone. We are going to dig deeper into the Lucia Ross Foundation. Tell us, what does your organization actually do on a day to day basis?"

"The core mission of Prisoner Freedom is evangelism. We work alongside other wonderful programs like Kairos and The Prison Fellowship. Kairos has concentrated programs to bring willing inmates to Christ. We compliment their teaching with day to day messages, prayers and mentoring inside the prisons. That's a bit tricky because there are strict rules against proselytizing in any government facility.

Priscilla faced the camera with a chuckle. "Don't hand me that tract, sister, or I'll call the cops."

"Exactly, but evangelism *can* exist in voluntary groups where inmates meet, and no one can stop one on one conversations. We began by teaching the Saints how to get

God into conversations, but we hardly rely on direct approaches like those anymore. We found that non believers are amazed by the transformation and happiness they see in their friends so now we just wait until they ask: 'what happened to you?' At that point our inmate believers can just tell them."

"I get it. You trick them into asking for something they don't want to hear. Let's go to something else. Tell the viewers something about your personal life. I understand you were in prison for murder yourself." She turned to her audience, made a face, then turned back to Esther. "You didn't do it, did you?"

Esther chuckled. "No, but God put me in that prison for His good purpose."

"Ms. Mason, seriously, those are hardened convicts in there. What use do they have for your religious stuff?"

Esther dropped her head, her look far away as she remembered back. "They all act tough during the day, Priscilla, but when the lights go off, their crying fills the night."

"Yeah, all guilty. We know. Except *you,* of course. You really think God sent you there?"

"His reasons may be hidden from us, but trusting God is always the best choice. While I was in prison, I began this ministry, found my purpose, and started writing. I also found my loving husband whom I absolutely adore."

Priscilla laughed. "Maybe we should recommend prison as a start for every young woman." She waited for the audience laughter. "I'm curious. Your bio says you met your husband while you were in prison. They're not going co-ed these days are they?"

"Bill was teaching a writing class for inmates." She looked out at the audience, grinned and batted her eyelashes. "When the course was over, he started visiting me."

"And how did you know he was the one? Was it because he bankrolled your appeal trial?"

The pain of that remark showed on Esther's face. "No, Ma'am. At first I thought he was just a concerned citizen because he could see I was getting beaten up in there, but I knew he really cared when he was so persistent. He even consented to doing my salvation prayer. Bill was happy to discover the Lord loved him and, of course, I don't think he minded that I fell in love with him too."

"We invited this loving husband of yours, but he declined. Is he flying around the country on foundation business?"

"No, his students are working on their college entrance exams, and some need tutoring. Besides, he wants to be with our children in the evening."

"You're telling us he's still a *teacher*? Doesn't he work for the foundation and take home a six figure salary?"

She chuckled. "No, his calling is teaching, but he does mentor the student group, 'Warriors for Christ'. Their High School mascot is a Greek warrior. Anyway, no one makes a big salary at our foundation, but we do employ lots of released prisoners."

"So, no high salaries except the CEO I assume."

"I peg my salary at eighty percent of what my husband earns teaching, and we publish our tax returns on our web site for all to see. It's a good way to insure trust in an organization. Maybe you should try it yourself, Priscilla."

She scowled and checked her notes. "We found out that your husband, William, was *fired* from his job three years ago but was later reinstated on a technicality after a lawsuit. Care to comment?'

Esther grinned. "Oh, my dear Bill…" She looked down and shook her head. "He mentioned God in his science class. One of the students recorded it and reported him."

"Ms. Mason, I'm sure you know that proselytizing is illegal in public school. It is offensive to those of other faiths or no faith."

"Yes, but he wasn't. He had quoted articles from Scientific American in 2013, the summations of the best of all human minds. One article said we remain puzzled by the true nature of subatomic particles. The other said we don't know how the "Big Bang" happened or why of *all* the possible universes that could have resulted, we were just 'lucky' to have one compatible with life."

"Then he tried teaching Creationist theory?"

"He simply said that since science does not know where we came from or what we're actually made of, the evidence is best explained by a creator with a vast intelligence beyond our capacity to understand."

"Like I said, a *Creationist.* The courts don't allow for such nonsense to be taught to our children. Why did this judge allow him to return?"

"The judge said that it is an integral part of science to declare what is unknown. He told opposing council that he would convict Bill of spreading false information only if the plaintiffs would offer proof that God does *not* exist."

Priscilla huffed, "You don't think Genesis is *literally* true, do you?"

"Genesis is the word of God and beautiful poetry. I recommend everyone read it."

"Poetry, perhaps," She grinned at the camera, "but nonsense for sure."

Esther regarded Priscilla with concerned compassion. "Cosmologists today note that the Genesis descriptions are 70% compatible with what we have so far discovered. Also it was written millennia before science even knew the world wasn't flat."

"But still, vague poetic notions, right?"

"No, pretty specific. While it would lack beauty, perhaps you would like Genesis to read like this: From His multidimensional world God balled up the sub atomics of matter and energy, precisely calibrating thousands of them to produce a completely unique universe. He then hurled them out to expand and develop into His new three dimensional universe, knowing that His work would result in our Earth, life, and ultimately mankind."

Esther gave Pricilla a silly cross-eyed grin to meet the thunderclouds forming over the host's eyes. "I'm really not that smart but Billy's been teaching me some science things."

"Well, I see we're almost out of time, but we did agree to let you make a closing statement about your organization."

She glanced into the camera with a pained smile. "Please promise me you won't try to lead the whole country to Jesus."

Esther's eyes widened. "But what *fun* that would be. Why not, Ms. Pris?"

Priscilla glanced from side to side. "Well, well we're a country that takes pride in *diversity*. Everyone can't be the same. We need to *tolerate* other points of view."

Esther laughed. "There's lots of points of view, but only one truth. Personally, I think it would be wonderful if we all had eternal life. Oh, I see our phone number and web site scrolling across the bottom of the screen. You can send a contribution, of course, but I want each listener to know we are also there to help you."

Esther's gaze focused beyond the camera. "There are many of you really hurting out there, many with lives crumbling, or with failing health. You do not have to fight your battle alone. Jesus is God and He deeply loves you, well beyond what you could imagine. All you need to do is reach out privately in prayer and ask: 'God, if you are there, please show me'. Call the number on the screen. You'll talk to someone who has been there, probably a former prison inmate. Share your troubles with us. We listen.

"When you have accepted the reality of our loving God, He will be with you and you'll find an inner joy you've never felt before. And God has a *specific* purpose just for you in His Kingdom, a purpose and a life that will give you true happiness. May the Lord bless each and every one of you. He's just waiting for you to…"

"And that's all the time we have. This has *certainly* been a unique day on Pris's Corner. We listen to *all* points of view, don't we? Tomorrow we'll have a Harvard professor who will explain why the world would be a better place if everyone got the same salary from the government. Sounds like a good idea to me, so be sure to tune in."

She smiled at the camera until the light went off, then tore her mike off, dropped it on the floor, and walked briskly off set without glancing at Esther. There was an awkward moment of silence. Esther stood up and looked over the studio audience. "I guess that means we're done?" They laughed.

The man with the wires and the clipboard hurried out, took Esther's microphone and ushered her off. Priscilla could be heard shouting at someone off stage. Kayla rushed up to Esther. "I'm so sorry, Esther, but Priscilla gets that way sometimes."

"I thought it all went fine, Kayla, but my hair feels like a rock."

Kayla giggled. "It's the spray hold. Without it, those stray hairs have a mind of their own under the lights. She just didn't want to hear your message, did she?"

"For some it would be harder than walking a camel through the eye of a needle. But, never mind. As long as you have me all gussied up, we should go out for lunch. I'm starved."

"Oh Ms—Esther, you really don't have to."

"Yes I do. We both should have a chance to do the thing we love most today, shouldn't we? I saw a cute bistro with outdoor tables about two blocks from here."

Kayla slipped off her work smock and grinned. "You know, you're just about the nicest person I've ever met."

As they headed out the door together Esther put her hand on Kayla's shoulder. "That's funny, I was just about to say the same thing about you."

AUTHOR BIO:

Pascal John Imperato, M.D. (Pen name, “John Pascal”)

Doctor Imperato has written fiction since junior high school. He was editor of his high school literary magazine, and went on to write short stories and take creative writing courses at Johns Hopkins. After an education in medicine he became the editor of his county medical newsletter. Writing and general science has long been a passion, now comfortably blended with being “born again” in the Lord.

Previously he published three novels collectively called “The Revelation Trilogy”. This story, he claims, is a joy filled work assignment from the Holy Spirit who always knows best.

www.ingramcontent.com/pod-product-compliance
Lightning Source LLC
Chambersburg PA
CBHW020821180626
46814CB00001B/53
9780692297735